Fenella Fang and the Wicked Witch

Ritchie Perry

Illustrated by Jean Baylis

Beaver Books

A Beaver Book

Published by Arrow Books Limited
20 Vauxhall Bridge Road, London SW1V 2SA

An imprint of Random Century Group

London Melbourne Sydney Auckland
Johannesburg and agencies throughout
the world

First published in 1989 by Hutchinson Children's Books
Beaver edition 1990

Text © Ritchie Perry 1989
Illustrations © Jean Baylis 1989

Made and printed in Great Britain by
Courier International Ltd,
Tiptree, Essex

ISBN 0 09 962260 2

FENELLA FANG
MEETS THE
WICKED WITCH

A BRIEF WORD ABOUT WITCHES

I really only want to talk about one witch, a particularly unpleasant specimen called Griselda. I ought to start, though, by explaining that there are all kinds of witches. There are nice ones and nasty ones, tall ones and short ones, fat ones and thin ones. A lot of them are incredibly ugly but it's best to remember one thing if you should meet a witch – always be polite, whatever she looks like. Even the nicest witches are very short-tempered and they're especially touchy about their appearance. It definitely isn't very sensible to make comments about the warts on their noses or the hairs on their chins. Do that and you probably won't be reading many more books. You'll be spending the rest of your life as a dog bowl or lavatory brush or something even worse. In any case, most witches don't have warts or hairy chins any more. They go to doctors and shave just like everybody else.

Another thing – don't expect to see witches flying around on broomsticks. Nowadays they usually prefer BMWs or Datsuns. If they need to fly anywhere, they travel on Concorde or a jumbo jet. You see, the trouble with broomsticks is that they're awfully wet and draughty in bad weather. Besides, the cats are always falling off when the witches loop the loop or make a sharp turn. That was why people used to talk about it raining cats and dogs; the cats had all fallen from witches' broomsticks. I don't know about the dogs but they might have been cats too – people can get very confused when cats have dropped on their heads from a great height.

Anyway, as I started to say, there are all kinds of witches but only one Witch Griselda.

Once upon a time she had been quite nice, but gradually she had been turning nastier and nastier – in fact, Griselda herself suspected that she had become absolutely horrid. Although this was certainly the way she felt, she couldn't be certain because she hadn't cast a spell for over seven hundred years. If you're thinking Griselda must have been a pretty lazy witch, you're wrong; she would have loved to use her magic, but unfortunately (or fortunately if she was as horrid as she thought), she couldn't – and this was the most unusual thing about her. As you must know, there are hundreds of witches who have turned people into toads. Griselda had even done it herself on a couple of occasions when she had climbed out of bed on the wrong side.* What made Griselda so different was that she was the only witch who had ever been turned into a toad herself.

In case you're wondering, this wasn't because one of her own spells had gone wrong. Like most witches, Griselda was very good at her job and it was most unusual for her to make a mistake. She had been turned into a toad by her husband, the mighty Wizard Yu-u-uck. His real name was Gilbert Anthony but all the wizards used to have nicknames. You can probably understand why. I mean, who could be serious about somebody who called himself the mighty Wizard Gilbert Anthony? He was given the nickname Yu-u-uck because his spells and potions tasted so horrid. Most of the other wizards had made theirs strawberry or banana flavoured but Griselda's husband had refused to do this. He said it weakened his magic and, in any case, he was running a wizardry not an ice-cream parlour.

To get back to what I was saying, Yu-u-uck had been quite fond of Griselda and, except for one brief moment, he had never wanted to turn her into a toad. In fact, Yu-u-uck had regretted what he had done the moment he saw his wife

---

*Witches who did have broomsticks, always kept them by their beds. If they got out of bed the wrong side, they'd stand on one end of the broomstick and the other end would spring up to hit them on the nose. This was very painful and put them in a bad mood all day.

hopping around on the floor. Unfortunately, there wasn't a great deal he could do about it. There are some spells which simply can't be removed and Yu-u-uck had happened to use one of them. The rules of magic are very strict about things like this. Yu-u-uck had said that Griselda would be a toad until she was kissed by a prince and once the words were out, he was stuck with them. He wasn't even allowed to put another spell on a prince and make him go around kissing every toad he saw. This would have been cheating and Yu-u-uck would have had his wizard's hat and spellbook taken away from him.

This was very hard luck on Griselda because the chances of a real prince kissing her while she was a toad were about three hundred thousand million to one against. I mean, can you imagine Prince Charles or Prince Andrew wasting their time kissing toads when they have Di and Fergie waiting for them back at the palace? Of course you can't. Or if you can, there must be something wrong with you. To tell the truth, Charles and Andrew wouldn't have wanted to kiss Griselda even before she had become a toad. She was the old-fashioned kind of witch with a very hairy chin. She had also had warts but not nearly so many as she had now she was a toad. Yu-u-uck had only married her because there weren't any other witches who could put up with his terrible tempers.

All the same, as I said before, Yu-u-uck had grown quite fond of Griselda and even after seven centuries he was still upset about the spell he had put on her. To be fair to him, it hadn't been entirely his fault. Griselda knew all about his temper and Yu-u-uck had often warned her that one day she would take one of her practical jokes a little bit too far. He had managed to keep his temper when he found his second-best cauldron was full of wriggling worms instead of the porridge he had been expecting for break-fast. He had even controlled it when he put on his wizard's hat and discovered just where the missing porridge was. It was the way Griselda had laughed at him that had finally made him lose control.

'Oh Yu-u-ucky,' she had cackled delightedly, 'you really are a sight. The porridge is all dribbling down behind your ears.'

The wizard hated being called Yu-u-ucky almost as much as he hated having hot porridge burning off his ears. It was then that his temper had snapped.

'Let's see how funny you find this, Grisly,' he'd shouted, waving his spellbook at her. 'DAOT EB, KAORC DNA SSIH, LLIT A ECNIRP EEHT SEOD SSIK.'

Although this would have been very difficult for you or me to shout, it was easy for a wizard like Yu-u-uck. Within the blink of an eye,

Griselda had become a toad and Yu-u-uck had started regretting what he'd done. As I've said, he was still regretting it seven centuries later, especially as there was nobody to warm his slippers in front of the fire or tidy up the cave. Just the same, Yu-u-uck was no longer hoping for some weird prince to turn his wife back into a witch again. He knew that Griselda's temper was almost as bad as his own and he didn't think that seven hundred years as a toad would have done anything to improve it. If she did ever become a witch again, Yu-u-uck suspected he might have a lot more to worry about than a hatful of porridge.

This was more true than Yu-u-uck knew. Griselda had discovered that being a toad was really boring. Apart from hiding under stones, croaking and generally hopping around, all she could do was plot her revenge. Griselda knew exactly what she intended to do if she ever had the chance, and thinking about this was her only pleasure. In fact, it was what she was doing when the two nasty little boys caught her. She was squatting there in the sun, thinking about all the horrible things she wanted to do to Yu-u-uck, when the net dropped over her.

'Got it,' the boy with the net shouted excitedly. 'There's your toad, Mike.'

'It's ever so ugly.'

'We didn't say anything about catching a pretty one.'

8

'I know, Alan, but—'

'No "buts",' Alan said firmly. 'A dare is a dare. You said you'd do it.'

Poor Griselda had no idea what was going to happen. The only thing she could be sure of was that she wouldn't enjoy it. She had met lots of nasty little boys while she had been a toad and it was always the same. They either poked her with sticks or played catch with her or dropped her out of trees to see if she could fly. Although she was enchanted and nothing could really hurt her, Griselda hated little children almost as much as she hated Yu-u-uck.

'Why couldn't toads have teeth and claws?' Griselda muttered savagely to herself. 'Then I'd teach the little monster a thing or two.'

The boy called Mike had picked her up and dropped her down the front of his shirt. The shirt was just as dirty and smelly as all the other shirts she had been dropped into.

'Urgh!' Mike shrieked. 'It's all horrible and slimy.'

It's not exactly a bundle of fun for me either, Griselda thought as the squirming boy bounced her around inside the shirt.

Fortunately, her ordeal didn't last very long. With a final shriek, Mike ripped open the buttons of his shirt, seized hold of Griselda and threw her to the ground. She was about to hop off into the bushes when the net unexpectedly descended on her again. This time it was being held by Mike.

'It's your turn now, Alan,' he said. 'Let's find out how brave you are.'

'What do you mean?'

'Yes, what do you mean, you little monster?' Griselda groaned, trying to push her way out of the net.

'I'm daring you to do what I did,' Mike explained with a grin. 'I want to see how much you enjoy having a slimy toad dancing all over your tummy.'

'I can't do that,' Alan objected. 'This is a brand new shirt. My Mum will kill me if I mess it up.'

'OK.' Mike was still grinning all over his face. 'I

dare you . . . I dare you to give the toad a kiss.'

'You must be joking,' Alan protested. 'I'm not kissing that ugly old thing.'

'Oh yes you are. It's a dare and if you don't do it, I'll tell everybody you're a chicken. Besides, you never know, that toad might turn into a beautiful princess when you kiss it.'

'That toad couldn't turn into a beautiful anything, not in a thousand years. Just look at it.'

Both of the boys were laughing as Alan reached under the net and picked Griselda up, squeezing her tightly so she couldn't slither free. He lifted her up and held her in front of his face.

'I was wrong,' Alan said. 'This toad isn't ugly. It's absolutely hideous.'

You're no oil painting yourself, pigeon-brain, Griselda thought, wishing she was a venomous toad and could spit poison into his face.

'Here goes then,' Alan said, closing his eyes and puckering his lips.

It was difficult to say who was surprised most by what happened next. There was a clap of what sounded like thunder; then Alan was flat on the ground with a fully grown witch sitting on his head. Griselda was as surprised as anybody but she was the quickest to recover from the shock. As soon as she realized what must have happened, she gabbled the first spell that came into her mind, just to check she wasn't dreaming. Poor Mike was still trying to understand how the hideous toad had turned into an even more hideous witch when he suddenly found himself shooting up into the air. About ten metres up he stopped just as suddenly and simply hovered there.

'I'm a witch,' Griselda cackled delightfully. She was bouncing up and down with glee, which wasn't doing a great deal for Alan's head. 'I'm really a witch again, not a stinking, croaking toad.'

'Waddayusay?'

Alan still had no idea what had happened. Although he could hear Mike screaming and he knew there was somebody bouncing up and down on his head, it was impossible to see anything with a witch sitting on his face. He couldn't speak very well either until Griselda shifted slightly to sit on his chest.

'Are you a prince?' she demanded, looking down at the terrified face.

'What?'

'You heard me.' Griselda playfully flicked Alan's nose with a bony finger, making tears spring into his eyes. To her delight, she was even more horrid than she had thought. 'You'd better learn to answer me quickly. Otherwise you'll end up as a cream cake at a birthday party.'

'I'm Alan Prince,' Alan babbled quickly. Nobody needed to tell him that Griselda was a witch and he was terrified. 'I live at 32 Blunsdale Road with my mum and dad and sister and two cats and a guinea pig and——'

'Alan Prince,' Griselda chortled happily, interrupting Alan before he could tell her about his bicycle and roller skates and conkers. 'A. Prince. I like that. Come to that, I like you, pigeon-brain. You've rescued me from a spell and I want to show how grateful I am.'

'You do?'

Alan didn't trust the evil smile on the witch's lips. Besides, she had just flicked his nose again and his eyes were watering more than ever.

'Oh yes. I want to give you something to remember me by. SRAE FO A YEKNOD SI YM LLEPS, TSUJ OT HCTAM RUOY ELBIRRET LLEMS.'

That's really wicked, Griselda thought gleefully, standing up so she could watch the donkey ears sprouting from either side of Alan's head. The boy helped me and I still did this to him. I really am awful.

'You said you liked me,' Alan wailed, feeling his new furry ears.

'But I do, my little pigeon-brain. That's why I didn't turn you into a cream cake. Anyway, I must be off now. My poor husband hasn't seen me for such a long time.'

'What about me?' a voice shouted from high above. 'Get me down from here.'

'Oh yes. We mustn't forget you, must we?'

Griselda quickly cast two more spells, one to stop Mike from ever changing his shirt and the other to make a huge patch of especially prickly thistles grow directly beneath him.

'You can come down whenever you like,' she said. 'All you have to do is shout "I love toads". Goodbye.'

Cackling evilly, Griselda walked off, heading for the cave where she used to live with the Wizard of Yu-u-uck. Be sure to remember her because you're going to meet Griselda again. For the moment, though, that's more than enough about witches. Let's begin our story.

One

The church clock was striking midnight as the vampire circled over the village, her great wings outstretched. The house she was watching was dark and silent and Fenella Fang's teeth flashed white in the moonlight as she allowed herself a smile of satisfaction. It was the same smile that had once won her the Miss Vampire of the Year award but although other vampires thought her quite beautiful, no human would have agreed with them. Those humans who had seen Fenella were reminded of something out of a nightmare. For some strange reason, humans just didn't appreciate her greenish skin, blood-red eyes and the huge teeth which could have ripped them into little shreds. And it was a human Fenella intended to visit tonight. The thought made her smile grow even broader.

She circled lower and lower, so low that her wings were almost brushing the chimney pot, and still there were no sounds from inside the house. This was just as Fenella had hoped and, silently, she landed on the roof, close to the attic window which stood ajar. The moon had just gone behind a cloud but this was no problem for Fenella. All vampires can see far better in the dark than any human can in broad daylight. At least, all vampires can apart from poor Claudius Crunch who couldn't see at all after he went out flying in a thunderstorm and was struck by lightning. After his accident he couldn't go anywhere without his six guide bats on leads to help him. Fenella's eyesight was perfect, though, and she could clearly see into the room through the flowered curtains which were billowing in the

breeze. The small shape of the girl curled up in the middle of the bed was clearly visible to her. At the foot of the bed there was the even smaller shape of the dog sleeping with his mistress. Somehow the dog must have sensed Fenella's presence because his head raised and he started to whimper.

'Quiet,' Fenella hissed fiercely.

Instantly, the dog was quiet. He stayed motionless on the bed as Fenella pulled the window wider open and stepped inside. Moving silently, she approached the bed, her huge shape towering over the sleeping child.

'Got you,' she snarled triumphantly, grabbing hold of the girl.

'Oh no, you haven't, Fenella,' a laughing voice said from behind the vampire. 'I've got you.'

Fenella had only just realized she was holding a bundle of rolled-up clothes when the girl jumped on her back, wrapping her arms and legs around the vampire. At the same time, the dog leapt up from the foot of the bed and began licking any part of Fenella he could reach. Although vampires didn't taste very nice, Spot was a friendly dog and any friend of his mistress was a friend of his.

What with one thing and another, it was some time before they had all sorted themselves out and were seated on the edge of the bed. Fenella had her arm around the girl who was cuddled up close against her. Although vampires don't smell much better than they taste, Sara was used to it. She found the musty, earthy odour rather comforting.

'It seems ages since I've seen you, Fenella,' she said, pressing even closer to the vampire's shroud.

As usual, Fenella felt cool to the touch but this didn't matter on a warm summer night.

'It's less than a munch*,' Fenella pointed out. 'Besides, I really have been awfully busy, Heinz Beans.'

This was the nickname Fenella had for Sara. There had been a time when she had thought it was the girl's real name. 'I haven't even had the time to fly over to Blood Castle.'

'What have you been doing?'

Fenella explained how she had been completely redecorating her crypt, rearranging all the cobwebs and spreading a thick new layer of dust. What with this and the new shrouds she had been sewing, the time had simply flown by. It was always the same in summer. The nights were so short it sometimes seemed to Fenella that she had hardly climbed out of her coffin before it was time to get back in again.

Once Fenella had finished, it was Sara's turn. She told her friend all about what she had been

*1 munch = 1½ human months

18

doing at school and how her father had taken her to the seaside. Last of all, she told Fenella about the woman who had moved into the house on the corner.

'She's really horrid,' Sara said. 'I feel frightened every time I go past her house.'

'Why? What has she done to you?'

'It's the way she looks at me.' Sara shivered and drew even closer to Fenella. 'It's as though she hates children and would like to do something horrible to me. And she has this big black cat which is just as bad. It sits on the wall and hisses at me every time I go past.'

'Does it really, dear?'

Fenella didn't understand what was unusual about this. Every cat she had ever met had arched its back and spat at her, the same way every dog except Spot had whined. Animals were almost as frightened of vampires as humans were.

'It does.' Sara still sounded upset. 'And I think the cat has already done something horrid to Spot. The first time he saw it, Spot wanted to play, just like he does with all cats. He chased it into Mrs Potion's garden. A few seconds later Spot came rushing out whining and yelping, with his tail between his legs.'

'Perhaps the cat didn't want to play. It probably scratched him.'

'Oh no, Fenella, it was something far worse

than that. There wasn't a mark on Spot – I know because I checked – but since then Spot has run away every time he's seen a cat. He's absolutely terrified of them.'

'Well, if this Mrs Potion and her cat do anything else to frighten you, just let me know.' Fenella sounded grim. 'I'll drop by one night and give them a little talking to. I'm sure they won't bother you any more after that.'

'Thank you, Fenella, but there's no need. I've decided not to walk past Mrs Potion's house any more. It's almost as easy to go the other way round. Anyway, I've wasted enough time talking about my new neighbour. What are we going to do tonight?'

'That's up to you, Heinz Beans. What would you like to do?'

'Well, tomorrow is a holiday.'

'What do you do with the holly? Prick each other with it or eat the berries?'

Fenella was interested. Even if she lived to be five thousand, she was sure she would never understand the strange customs humans had. It could be they even wore the holly, although this sounded rather uncomfortable.

'I'm not talking about holly the plant.' Sara was laughing. 'I mean a *holiday*.

'Oh.'

Poor Fenella was more confused than ever.

'It's a day when nobody has to go to work or

school or anything,' Sara explained. 'I don't have to get up early in the morning. It won't matter if I stay in bed all day.'

'Ah, I understand now, Heinz Beans.' Fenella was smiling as well. 'What you're saying is, you'd like me to fly you somewhere.'

'I was hoping we could do that.'

'Of course we can. Where would you like to go?'

'Well ...' Sara hesitated a moment, 'where I'd really like to go is Blood Castle. It seems ages since I last saw your Uncle Samuel and Igor. They wouldn't mind, would they?'

'You know they wouldn't,' Fenella told her. 'In fact, Uncle Samuel often talks about you. He says you're the only sensible human he's met apart from Igor. If we're going, you'd better climb aboard.'

It took Fenella a matter of seconds to change back into her bat form. Once she had, Sara scrambled on to her back. As she wrapped her arms around Fenella's neck, the little girl thought how lucky she was to have a real vampire for a friend.

Fenella's uncle, Samuel Suck, was the most famous of all the vampires. Although his younger brother, Dracula, was the one humans made all the silly films about, Samuel was far better known among other vampires. For a start, at the

21

age of 2323 he was easily the oldest of them all, and he was the only vampire who had to wear false teeth. But the main reason for his fame was that Samuel Suck was by far the greatest of all vampire inventors. It was Samuel who had done most of the work on HBS (Human Blood Substitute). He was the one who had invented SAPS, Safety Pockets which stopped vampires losing things while they were flying about the night sky. There had been countless other important inventions, and at the very moment that Fenella was talking with Sara, Samuel was putting the finishing touches to his latest idea. Ever since he had climbed out of his coffin that night, he had been hard at work in the dungeons of Blood Castle.

'I think that just about does it,' he said to himself, standing back to admire his handiwork.

The thick layer of dust on the dungeon floor looked smooth and undisturbed. There was no sign of the work he had been doing and Samuel smiled in satisfaction. As he only wore his false teeth at mealtimes, it was a rather gummy smile.

'Now to find if it works,' he went on. 'I'll need Igor's help for that.'

Igor was Samuel's servant and he had been made to stay out of the dungeons until his master had finished. However, he did know that Samuel was working on a new invention and this was enough to make him gloomy and nervous as he sat waiting in the Great Hall. Igor knew who would be testing the invention. It would be him and, like all great inventors, Samuel Suck wasn't always successful.

'And I always get the inventions that go wrong,' Igor muttered miserably. 'I know just what's going to happen. I'll get fried or drowned or frozen again.'

The very thought of being frozen again made Igor shiver. CHEATS* had been one of Samuel's greatest inventions. Vampires need to keep cool and, unlike Fenella and Samuel, many of them weren't lucky enough to have suitable accommodation for their coffins. What with all the new council estates and high-rise apartment blocks the humans were building, there simply weren't enough dank dungeons and crypts to go around. Some of the less fortunate vampires had suffered terribly during hot spells of weather and they had been delighted with CHEATS. With the refrigeration unit attached to their coffins, they were able to rest peacefully all day, no matter how hot it was outside. What they didn't know, though, was that at first the invention had worked a little too well. When it was first tested on Igor, he had spent four days and nights trapped inside a huge block of ice. Even after the ice had melted, it was another week before all

*Controlled Heating and Temperature Selector

Igor's goose-pimples had finally gone.

'I'm not going to do it,' Igor mumbled. 'I'll tell the Master to test it himself.'

One of the warts on Igor's head was itching and he scratched it with a filthy fingernail. There were a lot of warts on Igor's head, far more than any witch or toad had. There was also quite a lot of green mould and dandruff mixed in with the warts, which wouldn't have helped Igor to win a beauty competition. If there had been an ugly contest, it would have been a different story. In fact, he was so hideous that Igor only ever looked in a mirror to frighten himself when he had hiccups. Even Igor's mother and father hadn't been able to bear the sight of him. When he was a child, they made him wear a brown paper bag over his head all the time so he didn't make them feel sick. This was probably why Igor had grown warts and mould instead of hair. The bag he used had once contained sticky, cream buns. All the crumbs and goo couldn't have been very good for his skin.

Another thing which couldn't have helped was that Igor didn't ever wash. He had never learned when he was young because of the paper bag and now he was grown up he still didn't bother. This meant that Igor smelled rather ripe. To be honest, he stank to high heaven and you could smell him coming for about five minutes before he actually arrived. This was very useful for the people who lived in the village near Blood Castle. Provided they weren't suffering from a bad cold, they always had plenty of warning when Igor was on his way to do some shopping. It gave them plenty of time to lock themselves indoors or put on their blindfolds so they didn't have to look at him.

It wasn't just the warts and the mould which made Igor so ugly. He was ugly all over. In fact, he looked rather like somebody who had been made out of spare parts by someone who had had his eyes tightly closed at the time. Igor's eyes, nose and mouth were all squashed over to one side of his face while there was a single, huge ear on the other. As if this wasn't bad enough, his arms and legs appeared as though they should have belonged to several different people. None of them were the same length and whenever he went anywhere, Igor always tried to walk with one foot on the pavement and the other in the gutter. This was the only way he could keep himself level and walk in a straight line. His different-size arms weren't quite so much of a problem and Igor found his long arm rather useful. He could scratch his toes without having to bend down.

Although Igor seemed absolutely revolting to other humans, vampires thought he was remarkably handsome for a human being. As they were a greenish colour themselves, they found the mould especially attractive, and they didn't find his smell unpleasant either. Indeed, Samuel Suck considered himself particularly fortunate to have such a good servant. This was one reason there was a fond smile on his lips as he came into the Great Hall.

'Ah, there you are, Igor,' he said cheerfully. 'I've been looking everywhere for you. There's something I want you to do for me.'

'Is there, Master?'

Unlike Samuel, Igor didn't sound at all cheerful. He was pretty sure he knew what was coming.

'Yes, Igor. I've just finished another of my inventions. As a special treat, I'm going to let you be the very first to try it out.'

'I don't want to, Master.'

'You don't want to?' Samuel could hardly believe his ears.

'No, Master.'

'In Drac's name, why not?'

'Your inventions are always for vampires, Master. They're not meant for humans like me.'

'But this invention is *intended* for humans.' Now Samuel was smiling again. 'You'll love it, Igor.'

'Will I, Master?'

Igor had been tricked before and he still sounded doubtful. He couldn't forget the time Samuel had asked him if he wanted to try a

26

SALAD. This had been the occasion when Igor had nearly drowned in the moat around the castle. He had thought he would be getting something to eat, not being thrown off the battlements to test a Safety Landing Device.

'You will, Igor,' Samuel said enthusiastically. 'There's nothing for you to worry about at all.'

'I won't be drowned, Master?'

'No, Igor.'

'Or fried?'

'Of course not.'

'Or frozen into a block of ice?'

'I keep telling you, Igor. Nothing can possibly go wrong. It's more like a game than anything else. I call it COPS.'

'You mean Cops and Robbers, Master?'

For the first time, Igor was becoming interested. He liked playing games.

'No, it's just COPS, Igor. Come down to the dungeons with me and I'll explain how it goes.'

As Igor followed his master towards the dungeons, he couldn't rid himself of the terrible feeling that he had been tricked again. He would have been certain of it if he had known that COPS stood for Coffin Protection and Security.

'You're sure you know what to do, Igor?' Samuel asked, sitting up in his coffin.

'Yes, Master.' Igor was over by the dungeon steps, a large hammer in one hand and a sharpened piece of wood in the other. 'Once

you've closed the coffin lid, I try to creep up on you. If I can, I'm supposed to hammer this stake into your chest.'

'That's right.'

'You're certain that's what you want me to do, Master?'

'You needn't worry,' Samuel said. 'You won't get anywhere near the coffin before I know you're there. Anyway, I'm closing the lid now.'

The lid closed, Samuel flicked on the special switch he had fitted in the coffin and settled back comfortably in the damp earth. Perhaps COPS wasn't one of his greatest inventions but it was certainly going to help a lot of vampires to sleep easier in their coffins. It was something people didn't realize. Humans knew that they were frightened of vampires, mainly because they had those silly ideas about vampires drinking their blood. It simply didn't occur to them that vampires might be frightened of humans, and quite a lot of Samuel's friends and acquaintances were. They had these terrible daymares about humans sneaking up to their coffins while they were asleep to hammer stakes into them or shoot them with silver bullets. Although this couldn't kill vampires or even damage them seriously, it still wasn't a pleasant experience. Besides, the holes were a confounded nuisance. Poor Millicent Morsel had been caught so many times she was beginning to look like a Gruyère cheese.

Thanks to COPS, this was all about to change. From now on vampires would be able to rest easy in their coffins because they would have Coffin Protection and Security to guard them. With the control switch flicked to ON, Samuel knew he was perfectly safe. As soon as Igor came anywhere near, a flashing red light would start inside the coffin. Even if he didn't notice the light, Samuel would still be safe. Hidden beneath the thick dust on the floor was a human trap. There was no way Igor could avoid it and once he stepped on the trap, that would be the end of the game. No human was going to cause any trouble while he was imprisoned in a net some twenty metres above the dungeon floor. Igor wouldn't be hurt at all but the net would certainly be a big surprise for him. The thought brought a smile to Samuel's face. He could just imagine the expression on his servant's face as he went shooting up into the air in the net.

'GOT YOU, MASTER,' Igor shouted, throwing open the lid of the coffin.

Quick as lightning, Igor reached into the coffin to position the stake on Samuel's chest, then raised the hammer high in the air. The hammer was already descending before the startled Samuel realized what was happening and managed to grab hold of Igor's wrist. Samuel had lasted for over two thousand years without any holes in his body and he didn't want to start collecting them now.

'What do you think you're doing?' he demanded angrily.

'I'm only doing what you told me, Master.'

'Well, you must be cheating,' Samuel said, sitting up in his coffin.

However, Samuel could plainly see that Igor hadn't been cheating at all. His footsteps were clearly visible in the dust and he had walked straight across the spot where the trap was concealed. Yet there had been no flashing red light and Igor certainly hadn't been scooped up in the net.

'That's very strange,' Samuel muttered,

scratching his head in bewilderment.

'What's strange, Master?'

'Oh, nothing, Igor. Will you just go over and stand there for a moment.... Yes, that's right. Just stop there.'

Igor was standing right over the net and still nothing was happening. Samuel tried waggling the control switch but this didn't make any difference at all.

'What do you want me to do now, Master?'

'Try jumping up and down on the spot.'

Igor jumped up and down. Although he had no idea why he was doing this, he was used to obeying unusual commands. It was something you soon became used to when you worked for a vampire.

'It's all right, Igor. You can stop now.'

The COPS still hadn't worked and Samuel was puzzled.

'I don't understand it,' he muttered as he climbed out of the coffin.

'What don't you understand, Master?'

'Why my invention doesn't work. I was sure it would.'

'What was supposed to happen, Master?'

'I'll show you.' Samuel walked across to stand beside Igor. 'There's a human-trap hidden under the dust, right where you're standing. It's to catch any humans who creep up on a vampire during the day.'

'Is the flashing red light part of the trap, Master?'

'What flashing red light?'

'The one I can see reflected in the lid of your coffin, Master.'

As soon as he looked across, Samuel could see it too.

'Why,' he said proudly, 'perhaps COPS is working after—'

Samuel didn't have the chance to finish because he was right. His invention *was* working. Levers were levering and pulleys were pulleying and the net which had been hidden beneath the dust was hidden no longer. It had sprung up around Samuel and Igor, trapping them as they were lifted swiftly towards the vaulted roof of the dungeon.

'It works, Igor,' Samuel shouted excitedly. 'It really works.'

'Whoopee, Master.'

Igor wasn't nearly so excited as Samuel, especially as his head had banged painfully against the dungeon roof. He didn't enjoy dangling high in the air with his arms and legs sticking out through the holes in a net.

'Just think,' Samuel went on. 'From now on all vampires will be able to rest peacefully in their coffins, knowing they're safe.'

'I can think of one who won't be able to, Master.'

'Who, Igor?'

'You, Master?'

'What are you talking about?'

There were occasions when Samuel really did wonder about Igor. Some of the things he said were incredibly stupid.

'Well, Master, where exactly is the switch to lower the net?'

'In my coffin, of course.'

'That's what I meant, Master. You won't be able to rest peacefully in your coffin because you'll be stuck up here with me.'

'I hadn't thought of that.'

Igor had and he was beginning to panic.

'We're going to die, Master,' he moaned. 'We'll be stuck up here for ever. We'll starve to death.'

'Don't be so silly, Igor,' Samuel said severely. 'Stop making such a dreadful fuss. Vampires never die and we can go without food for ages and ages.'

'But I'm not a vampire, Master.' Igor was more upset than ever. 'I'm a human and my tummy is starting to rumble already.'

It really was too much. Igor had been drowned, frozen and fried by his master's inventions. Now it looked as though he was going to be starved as well.

Two

'What in Drac's name are you two doing up there?' Fenella asked.

Fenella and Sara had arrived at Blood Castle to find there was no one about. It wasn't until they had thought to look in the dungeons that they had discovered Samuel and Igor.

'We're starving,' Igor babbled. 'We're starving to death.'

'Don't be so silly,' Samuel told him. 'We've only been here for about thirty snaps*.'

'But why are you up there?'

'I'm afraid one of my inventions went a little wrong,' Samuel explained.

'As usual,' Igor muttered under his breath.

He didn't mutter quietly enough.

'What did you say, Igor?' Samuel demanded fiercely.

'Nothing, Master.'

'That's just as well for you.'

*1 snap = 1 human minute

Although Samuel was fond of Igor, he was always very sensitive about his inventions. Besides, he was rather tired of being cooped up in the net with his servant for company. Igor seemed unable to keep still and every time he moved, some nobbly part of him would dig into Samuel.

'How are you going to get down, Uncle?'

'That's easy, dear. In fact, little Sara can do it for me if she likes. If she goes to look in my coffin, she'll see a flashing red light.'

'I can see it.'

Sara had already run across to the coffin.

'Can you see the two little levers beside the light, dear?'

'Yes, Mr Suck.'

'Well, if you press the bottom one, the net will open and I can fly down.'

'But, Master—' Igor began.

'Oh do be quiet, Igor,' Samuel told him. 'I'm tired of your whining.'

'But, Master—'

'Quiet, I told you,' Samuel roared.

Old as he was, Samuel could still sound very fierce when he wanted to, and Igor was shocked into silence. In any case, Sara had already pressed the lever. The bottom of the net opened at once and, as soon as he was free, the old vampire glided gracefully towards the floor. Igor wasn't quite so graceful. As he didn't have any wings, he simply fell, hurtling towards the stone-flagged floor.

'Help!' he screamed. 'I'll crush my cranium.'

For once it seemed as though Igor was right. He was tumbling head first towards the floor and, with Fenella and Sara watching helplessly, it seemed nothing could save him. Then, at the very last moment, Samuel swooped underneath him, catching Igor before his head struck the flagstones. Cackling happily, Samuel gently deposited Igor on the floor.

'You didn't really think I'd let you hurt yourself, did you?' he asked, still chortling.

'Of course not, Master,' Igor lied, trembling all over.

'Anyway,' Samuel went on, turning to Fenella and Sara, 'thank you very much for your assistance but there are obviously one or two minor adjustments I have to make to my invention. I do hope you won't think I'm rude if I fix them now before I join you.'

'That's perfectly all right, Uncle. Igor can look after us while you're busy. If we talk to him nicely, we might even be able to persuade him to join us in a game.'

'Oh yes please, Mistress.'

The trembling had suddenly stopped and a great smile was splitting Igor's face. This was one of the reasons he enjoyed Sara's visits. He had never been able to play any games while he was a boy because he had never had any friends.

Playing hide and seek wasn't as easy for Igor as it was for most people. For a start, he always had to be the one who did the seeking. If Igor tried to hide himself, he was found straight away. All Sara had to do was follow her nose and Igor's smell led her directly to him. Even when he was doing the counting, Igor still had problems because he couldn't count up to three, let alone a hundred. Although Igor's parents had tried to send him to school, all the other children had run off screaming as soon as they saw his face and so had the teachers. Wearing his paper bag to school hadn't worked either because everybody else said his smell made them feel ill. So poor Igor had had to stay at home and had never learned to count. When they played together, Sara had to help him by counting a hundred of his pet beetles into a jar. Igor slowly dropped them one by one into another jar before he started seeking.

Normally Igor and Sara were the only ones who played but, as Samuel was still busy in the dungeons, Fenella had decided to join in. While Igor was busily transferring his beetles from one jar to another, she and Sara had run to one of the rooms in Blood Castle's highest turret.

'Igor will never find us here,' Sara panted
happily.

'Let's hope not.' Fenella was enjoying herself.
'Look, you go over there and hide in the
cupboard. I'll see if I can squeeze on top of the
wardrobe.'

It was a tight fit and Fenella found it difficult
getting behind the pile of empty boxes on top of
the wardrobe. However, she had just about
managed it when Sara called to her from the
other side of the room.

'Hush, child,' Fenella whispered. 'Igor will
have finished dropping beetles by now. We don't
want him to hear us.'

'But it's important, Fenella. There's already somebody hiding in the cupboard. It's a Red Indian.'

'A Red Indian? Whatever are you talking about?'

Fenella wasn't quite sure what a Red Indian was. Besides, Uncle Samuel would have told her if there had been any guests staying at the castle.

'Come down and look, Fenella. He's fast asleep.'

It only took Fenella a second to get down from the wardrobe. When she looked in the cupboard she saw that Sara had been telling the truth. The stranger inside was quite tall, although he wasn't as tall as Fenella, and his only clothing was a pair of deerskin trousers. However there was a beartooth necklace around his neck and he had a headdress of feathers. There were also patterns drawn on his face. Although Fenella thought he looked rather fine, there was one thing which puzzled her.

'He's brown,' she said.

'I know.'

'So he's a Brown Indian.'

'No, Fenella. He's a Red Indian.'

Fenella was about to tell her how silly this was when the girl suddenly grabbed hold of her arm.

'Fenella,' she whispered, her eyes opened wide in amazement. 'I can see right though his body.'

'Of course you can.' Fenella failed to understand why Sara was so surprised. 'That's because he's a ghost.'

'A gh-gh-ghost?'

Despite herself, Sara took a step backwards.

'There's no need to be frightened, Heinz Beans. He won't hurt you.'

'Are you sure?'

Even with Fenella there beside her, Sara felt a little nervous. She had never met a ghost before.

'Of course I am. Vampires and ghosts have always been friends. Nearly always, anyway.'

As Fenella was speaking, the ghost opened his eyes. When he saw her standing in front of him, the Red Indian raised a hand in greeting.

'How,' he said in a deep voice.

'How what?' Fenella demanded.

'Justum how.'

'That doesn't make sense.'

'It's what Red Indians always say,' Sara explained.

She was too curious to feel frightened any more. In any case, the ghost seemed harmless enough.

'How,' the Red Indian said again.

'You're getting really boring,' Fenella told him. 'Isn't there anything else you can say? Like your name?'

'Okey-dokey,' the ghost said obligingly. 'Meum Geronimo. Meum greatum chiefum.'

'Youum greatum painum in neckum,' Fenella

said. 'Dracula's teeth, can't you even speak properly?'

'Of course I can,' Geronimo told her. 'It's just that all you white folk expect us Red Indians to speak stupid.'

'I'm not a white folk, I'm a green folk and I far prefer being able to understand you.'

'Okey-dokey. No sweat.'

He didn't have the opportunity to say anything more because at that moment Igor rushed into the room, a big smile on his face. There were also a few cobwebs draped behind his ear. He had been searching the wine cellar when he had heard the voices in the turret.

'Caught you both,' he shouted delightedly. 'I found you almost straight. . . .'

Then Igor stopped. He had just caught sight of the figure in the cupboard.

'Who's that?' he demanded.

'His name is Geronimo,' Sara told him. 'He's a ghost.'

'A ghost?' Igor glared at Geronimo. 'We don't want any of those nasty creatures here at Blood Castle.'

As he spoke, Igor slammed the cupboard door shut. This was a complete waste of time since Geronimo drifted straight out through the closed door.

'Have you nearly recovered from your accident?' Geronimo asked politely.

41

'What?' Igor didn't understand what the ghost was talking about.

'Were you run over by a steamroller?'

'I haven't been run over by anything.'

'Perhaps an elephant stamped on your head then. Something terrible must have happened to make you look the way you do.'

With a cry of anger, Igor hurled himself at Geronimo. This was even more of a waste of time than slamming the cupboard door had been. As

there was nothing solid for him to grab hold of, he simply went straight through the ghost and banged his nose on the wall. Before he could do anything else, Fenella grabbed hold of Igor by the ear, lifted him from the ground and gave him a shake.

'Ouch,' he yelped. 'That hurts.'

'Good,' Fenella said fiercely. 'I won't have you behaving like that with a guest.'

'Didn't you hear what he said to me, Mistress?'

'That's no excuse.' Fenella gave Igor another shake. 'You remember to be polite.'

'That's right,' Geronimo said with a smirk. 'Listen to what the lady says.'

'As for you,' Fenella continued, swinging round to face the ghost and dropping Igor in a heap on the floor, 'You watch your language. Igor is a friend of mine.'

'Okey-dokey,' Geronimo said, raising both hands in apology. 'I won't mention how ugly he is again.'

'He's at it again, Miss Fenella,' Igor was outraged. 'He keeps saying I'm ugly.'

'I'm sorry, I'm sorry. It was a slip of the tongue.'

'Make sure it's the last,' Fenella told him. 'I don't want Igor upset.'

'It won't happen again. I promise.'

Geronimo hadn't promised not to pull faces, though, and he pulled an especially unpleasant one as soon as Fenella turned away. Igor simply glared and rubbed his sore ear. He was determined to get the ghost out of Blood Castle at the first possible opportunity.

When they went downstairs, they discovered that Samuel was still busy in the dungeons. While they were waiting for him, Geronimo explained how he had come to be in the cupboard in the turret. As Sara had guessed, he was a Red Indian ghost but, like all the rest of his kind, he lived in New York. Apparently it was completely impossible to haunt a wigwam or a tepee. Not only was there no room but the owners were always moving them somewhere else while the ghost wasn't looking.

'If you live in New York, what are you doing here at Blood Castle?' Fenella asked.

'White man givum too muchum firewater.'

'What does that mean?'

'Toadstool gin,' Geronimo explained. 'I went to a party at a friend's house. When I went to catch the Staten Island ferry to go home, I had a little bit of bad luck.'

'What kind of bad luck?'

'I went on board the QE2 by mistake. The next thing I knew I was here in England.'

'Why didn't you just stay on board and go back to New York?'

'Yes, why didn't you?' Igor muttered.

'Greatum waterum givum badum tumtum.'

'Speak properly,' Fenella snapped.

'I'm sorry. I keep forgetting. What I meant to say was that I was seasick.'

'Seasick?'

This wasn't a word Fenella recognized.

'It's the movement of the water, Fenella,' Sara broke in excitedly. 'I was seasick once when I went on the ferry to Boulogne. It was awful. I felt as though I was going to die.'

'It's even worse if you're a ghost,' Geronimo told her. 'I felt as if I was going to live. I shall never, ever go on a ship again. Besides, I like it over here in England.'

'Well you can't stay here,' Igor told him. 'The castle is full.'

'Oh, that's a terrible fib, Igor.' Now she had recovered from her nervousness, Sara was enjoying talking with a ghost. 'There's plenty of room.'

'Yes, stop being so horrid, Igor,' Fenella told him. 'I don't know what's got into you tonight. We can't just throw Geronimo out.'

'Of course we can't. The unexpected interruption made all of them swing round in surprise. They hadn't heard Samuel come into the Great Hall. 'Igor knows the laws of vampiredom as well as I do.'

'Yes, Master.'

Igor hung his head in shame. This way he

didn't have to look at the smirk on Geronimo's face.

'What's Uncle Samuel talking about?' Sara whispered to Fenella.

'There was a time, long long ago when vampires and ghosts weren't very friendly,' Fenella explained. 'They were always arguing, usually about who should live where. It was all very silly and in the end an agreement was reached. One of the most important decisions to be reached was that no vampire should ever refuse shelter to a ghost.'

'And no ghost would ever turn out a vampire,' Geronimo added.

'So Geronimo can stay here, then?'

'It's the law,' Samuel told her.

'I'm glad,' Sara said. 'I like Geronimo.'

'I don't,' Igor muttered.

'Don't be such a spoilsport. I bet Geronimo is ever so good at hide and seek.'

Igor simply snorted and said nothing. One thing was for sure, though. If the dratted ghost did play hide and seek, he'd have to find his own beetles. Igor certainly wasn't lending him any of his.

Three

If anybody was to blame, it was Manfred Murgatroyd. Sara was playing with Spot in the garden,
throwing the ball for him to catch and bring
back, when Manfred arrived. For a while Manfred had simply stood and watched, laughing out
loud when Spot leapt high in the air to catch the
bouncing ball.

'I wish I was allowed to have a pet,' he said at
last.

'Perhaps you will be when you're a bit older.'

Manfred was only five and his parents were
very strict with him.

'Perhaps.' Manfred sounded doubtful. 'Can I
throw the ball for Spot, please?'

'You can if you're very careful,' Sara told him.

Throwing was one of the things which Manfred wasn't very good at. Although he could
throw a long way, he was never quite sure which
direction the ball was going in.

'I will be,' Manfred promised, reaching out to
take the ball.

'You'd better be,' Sara warned him. 'This is Spot's favourite ball. Stand with your back to the hedge. That way the ball won't go into the road.'

Once he had the ball in his hand, Manfred stood with his back to the hedge and threw the ball down the garden. At least, he would have done if he had remembered to let go of the ball at the right moment. But he didn't. He kept hold of the ball too long and instead of it flying down the garden, it sailed backwards over Manfred's head, over the hedge and out into the road.

'Oh, Manfred. I told you to be careful.'

'I'm sorry, Sara. I'll go and fetch it for you.'

Unfortunately, he didn't get the chance. At that moment Mrs Murgatroyd opened the door of her house across the road.

'Manfred,' she called. 'You'd better come in now. It's time for lunch.'

For a moment, Manfred hesitated, uncertain what to do. Then Sara gave him a little push.

'Go on,' she said. 'You'd better go home before you get into trouble. I'll fetch the ball.'

In fact, she expected Spot to fetch it for her. There was a hole in the hedge just big enough for him to slip through and he had gone rushing after the ball almost the moment Manfred had thrown it. Although this wasn't something Spot was supposed to do, Sara wasn't too worried. There was hardly ever any traffic along the road where she lived. And when a car did come, you could hear it long before it actually arrived.

All the same, Spot did seem to be taking rather a long time. Sara walked to the gate and looked down the road. It was deserted. There was no sign of Spot or the ball anywhere.

'Spot,' she called. 'Come on. Good boy.'

There was no response. Nothing moved along the road.

'Spot,' Sara called again, louder this time. 'Where are you?'

There was still no sign of him and now Sara was beginning to worry. Spot was normally a very obedient dog. She only had to call him and he would be at her side in a flash. Even if he was chasing a cat, he would stop immediately when Sara called him.

Thinking about cats reminded Sara of Mrs Potion and she looked down towards the corner where the horrid old woman lived. It came as a shock to see the black cat sitting there in the gateway. Although it was some distance away, it seemed to be staring back at her and, suddenly, Sara knew exactly what had happened. The road sloped downhill all the way to the corner. When Manfred had thrown the ball back over his head and over the hedge, it had bounced and rolled all the way down the hill into Mrs Potion's garden. Spot, of course, would have chased after it. Even though the cat had frightened him so badly, he would have gone into the garden because it was

49

his special ball and he wouldn't want to lose it. So he had gone into Mrs Potion's garden and then …and then …. Sara didn't know what had happened then but for some reason she was shivering and her arms were covered with goosebumps. Whatever had happened, Spot hadn't come out again.

'Spot.' Now there was a note of desperation in the girl's voice. 'Here, boy.'

But Spot didn't come. Slowly, ever so slowly, Sara started to walk down the hill. She was frightened but she knew she had to go. Something bad had happened to Spot and he was her dog. She couldn't just leave him. If her dad had been at home, Sara would have asked him to go with her. Unfortunately, he was at work and it was no good asking Mrs Wipeit, the housekeeper. She would be far too busy washing the curtains or dusting the sideboard or Hoovering the lawn.

Each step seemed to be more of an effort. Although the sun was shining brightly, Sara felt deathly cold, and twenty metres from the gate she simply couldn't go any further. The black cat was still sitting in the gateway, watching her approach, and for once it wasn't hissing at her. It almost seemed to be smiling at her. For some reason, Sara found this the most frightening thing of all.

'Come on, Sara,' she said, speaking fiercely to

herself. 'You're imagining things. Mrs Potion is only a little old lady, however horrid she looks. She isn't going to eat you and nor is that silly cat.'

This wasn't enough to start her walking again. Brave as she was, Sara might even have turned back if she hadn't put her hand in the pocket of her jeans and felt the whistle. Although she had never used it, she took it everywhere with her. It was a very special whistle, given to her by Fenella. She only had to blow it and her friend would be with her in a matter of seconds.

Sara was still nervous but with the whistle clutched tightly in her hand, she didn't feel nearly so alone. While the cat watched, she began walking again, along the last few metres of pavement, past the cat and on to the path leading

to Mrs Potion's house. The cat didn't move until Sara had gone by. Then it stood up, stretched and followed her. Sara could hear the soft pad, pad of its paws on the gravel behind her.

It was a long path, winding through the trees and shrubs which almost filled the garden. Under the trees, it was very dark and very silent. No birds sang above in the branches. No small animals moved among the bushes. Sara was becoming frightened again and she might even have turned back if she hadn't seen the ball, lying in some leaves at the side of the path. If the ball was there, so was Spot. Keeping tight hold of the whistle, Sara hurried up the steps leading to the house and rang the doorbell.

'What do you want, child?'

The voice was so unexpected, coming from behind her, that it made Sara jump. When she turned, she saw Mrs Potion standing at the bottom of the steps, the black cat rubbing against her legs. The old woman looked even more frightening close to than she did at a distance.

If she had much more hair on her top lip, she'd have a proper moustache, Sara thought to herself. Just look at that wart on the end of her nose. I've never seen anything like it. And those eyes—

Sara didn't want to think about Mrs Potion's eyes any more because they were the most scary thing of all. They seemed to be looking right inside Sara, as though they were X-rays. Sara realized she was shivering again.

'Don't just stand there gawping like an idiot, child.' It was a harsh, unpleasant voice and somehow it sounded evil. 'I asked you what you wanted.'

'I'm sorry, Mrs Potion.' Frightened as she was of the old woman, Sara kept her voice firm. She also remembered to be polite. 'I'm looking for a dog.'

'What do you think this is? A pet shop? Besides, I don't like dogs. They're nasty, un-pleasant creatures.'

Although Mrs Potion hadn't actually said so, Sara knew she didn't like children either. It was there in Mrs Potion's eyes.

'It's my dog I'm looking for,' Sara explained. 'I think it came into your garden.'

'You should keep the little beast on a lead.'

'I know and I'll make sure it doesn't happen again. Have you seen him, please?'

'That all depends.' Mrs Potion appeared to be amused for some reason. 'Is he a little black and white dog?'

'That's right.'

'Is he wearing a brown, leather collar?'

'Yes.'

'And does the collar have a name tag on it saying SPOT?'

'Yes, that's him.'

'In that case, I'm afraid I can't help you. I've never seen a dog like that in my life.'

Mrs Potion thought this was so funny, she cackled out loud, and the cat gave a miaow which made it sound as though it was laughing too. Sara was too angry and too worried about Spot to think about being frightened any more.

'Yes you have seen him,' she said fiercely. 'I know you have and I want him back now.'

'You do, do you?'

Mrs Potion wasn't cackling any more.

'Yes, I do. And if I don't get him back, there's going to be trouble.'

'What do you mean? Trouble?'

'If anything has happened to Spot, you'll soon find out.'

Sara was clutching Fenella's whistle tighter than ever.

'Will I, my little pigeon-brain?' As she spoke, Mrs Potion smiled an evil, unpleasant smile which showed her crooked, yellowish teeth and made Sara shrivel inside. 'Well, I wouldn't want that to happen. Perhaps I'd better take you to your precious Spot after all. Come on. He's this way.'

The old woman had turned on her heel and started walking round towards the back of the house, her cat following close behind. Reluctantly, with dread in her heart, Sara followed her too.

* * *

'Dracula's teeth,' Fenella moaned, rubbing her head. 'That hurt.'

She had been fast asleep when the whistle sounded and she had sat up so suddenly that she had banged her head against the coffin lid. Fenella knew at once that it must have been Sara's vampire whistle because it was the only one in existence. Fenella also knew that Sara must be in trouble. She had never, ever used the whistle before and she was far too sensible to blow it unless there was a real emergency. Besides, the whistle had been blown so hard that Fenella's ears were still ringing. It had been a cry for help and Fenella knew it.

Without any more ado, she pushed open the lid and climbed out of her coffin. Although it was pleasantly dark inside the crypt, Fenella knew it was still daylight outside. There had been a time when no vampire could venture outside until after dark but, thanks to Uncle Samuel, this was a thing of the past. He had invented a special cream to protect the skin and some anti-glare goggles to cover the eyes. Fenella had used them several times before and she intended to use them now.

Running round the coffin, she pulled open the drawer where the cream and goggles were kept. The cream was there, just as she had expected, but there was no sign of the goggles. Muttering under her breath, Fenella started pulling open the other drawers, rummaging among the shrouds and cloaks. Then she went through them all again, more carefully this time. It was a waste of effort. The goggles were nowhere to be found and there was no question of her leaving the crypt without them. Even the weakest ray of sunlight would be enough to damage her sensitive eyes.

'Creaking coffinlids,' Fenella cursed. 'Where can they be?'

They definitely weren't in any of the coffin drawers. Fenella had even emptied them all to make sure.

'What can I have done with them?' she muttered, becoming increasingly annoyed with herself. 'It's not like me to lose things. I'm no Gerty Gore.'

As soon as she mentioned the name, Fenella remembered. The goggles weren't lost; they had been borrowed. Gerty Gore had come visiting her one night and stayed chatting for so long that it was daylight before she decided to leave. Of course, being Gerty, she had forgotten to bring her own goggles with her. She had had to borrow Fenella's pair and, being Gerty, she hadn't yet returned them.

'Oh, stakes and silver bullets.' It wasn't often that Fenella swore but she did so now. 'I shan't be able to leave until it's dark.'

Her sole consolation was that Sara had only blown the whistle once and Fenella decided this was a good sign. It probably meant Sara wasn't in any serious trouble. A few moments later, Fenella changed her mind. Perhaps Sara had only been able to blow the whistle once. That would mean she was in really terrible trouble.

Poor Fenella didn't know what to think and she was far too upset to even consider going back to her coffin to rest. She paced impatiently backwards and forwards in the crypt instead, kicking the rats out of her way and imagining all the dreadful things that could have happened to her friend. The moment it was dark, she was off, flying faster than she had ever flown before. She was travelling at such speed that if any keen-sighted human had glanced up he would simply have seen a dark blur against the night sky.

It was too early for Sara to be in bed and, once she reached her destination, Fenella circled above the house, wondering what she ought to do. It was a long time since the whistle had summoned her and everything seemed normal enough down below. At least, it seemed as normal as anything to do with humans ever did. All the downstairs lights were on and horrible sounds were drifting out through the windows. Fenella knew that this was what humans thought of as music. She could never understand why they didn't listen to decent tunes, songs like her own favourites *Fangs for the Memory* and *All you need is teeth*.

Before she decided what to do, Fenella dropped down to the roof and peered in through the window of Sara's room. As she had feared, it was empty. Sara wasn't there and nor was Spot. The next step was to check downstairs and Fenella swooped down into the garden. Moving as quietly as only a vampire knew how, she went round the house, peeping in at all the windows. Once again there was no sign of either Sara or Spot. The only person at home was Mr Parker, Sara's father. Fenella recognized him from the photograph upstairs in Sara's bedroom. The music had stopped now and he was sitting in front of some kind of magic box which was showing him moving pictures. Fenella had never seen anything quite like it before and she watched through the window for a while. However, she soon became bored. All the pictures showed was a lot of silly men in short trousers who were chasing a ball around a field and kicking each other. The strange things humans did never ceased to amaze her.

So far Fenella wasn't any closer to solving the mystery about Sara. She didn't even know where to begin looking. The only person who could help her was inside the house but Fenella could hardly walk in and ask him. This was another silly thing about humans. Whenever they saw a vampire they screamed or fainted or did something equally stupid. Fenella never made that kind of fuss when she saw a hideous human.

It was while she was standing outside the window, wondering what to do, that Fenella noticed the washing line in the next garden. Slowly a big smile spread across her face. Perhaps she could just walk in and ask Mr Parker after all.

Mr Parker was on the edge of his seat with excitement. It was one of the best matches he had seen for a long time and the last thing he wanted was for the doorbell to ring.

'Drat and double drat,' he muttered, his eyes still glued to the television set.

He hoped that if he stayed where he was, the person outside would decide to go away. He should have known better. After a few seconds his visitor put a finger back on the doorbell and kept it there. Cursing under his breath, Mr Parker hurried through to answer the front door.

At first he thought somebody must have bricked it in while he was watching television. Then he realized that his visitor was very large, almost filling the doorway. She was also very strange. As far as Mr Parker could tell, she was wearing a flowered dressing gown which was at least three sizes too small, there was a striped bathtowel wrapped around the lower part of her face and a large pair of blue knickers on her head. Although most of her face was hidden, she

seemed to have put something on her skin to turn it a greenish colour. Even more weird, her eyes were very red and seemed to flash in the semi-darkness. All in all, she was so strange and menacing that Mr Parker nearly slammed the door in her face.

'Is it Hallowe'en?' he asked weakly, taking a step backwards.

'No, I'm Fenella.'

Fenella had no idea what the man was talking about.

'Oh, are you?' Mr Parker said out loud.

She's not just weird, he thought to himself. She's got a few screws loose as well.

'I'm sorry to disturb you,' Fenella told him. 'I was wondering if I could have a few words with your daughter.'

'I'm afraid you must have come to the wrong house, Mrs Fenella.' Suddenly Mr Parker was feeling much better. 'I don't have a daughter.'

'Don't have a daughter?' The towel had slipped and Mr Parker noticed what large, sharp teeth his visitor had. They made him go all wobbly inside. 'I'm talking about Sara.'

'It's still the wrong house, I'm afraid. I live here on my own.'

Fenella leaned forward to take a closer look at Mr Parker, not noticing how her musty, earthy smell made him shrink back. Yes, there was no doubt about it. She was definitely talking to Sara's father, the same man she had seen in the photograph beside her friend's bed.

'If you live here on your own, whose is the attic room?' Fenella asked.

'There isn't an attic room,' Mr Parker told her. 'You must be thinking of some other house.'

'But—'

Mr Parker didn't allow her the chance to finish.

'I'm afraid I must go now, Mrs Fenella. I really am very busy. Goodnight.'

After he had closed and locked the front door, he left a very puzzled Fenella standing on the doorstep. She was also more worried than ever.

* * *

Although Fenella had never understood human ways, she knew enough to realize that Mr Parker's behaviour had been very odd. Why had he said he didn't have a daughter when he did? Why had he said there was no attic room when everybody could see it? Fenella felt quite proud of the clever way she had dressed up as a human but this was her only cause for satisfaction. Mr Parker had left her with more unanswered questions than she had started with.

Once she had returned the borrowed clothes to the washing line, Fenella flew up to the roof to make absolutely certain there hadn't been a mistake. The attic room was there, just as it had always been, and the window was ajar. Fenella slipped quickly inside and went across the bed-side table to check the photograph. As she had expected, there was no doubt about it. The man in the photograph was the same man she had spoken to downstairs.

It was all most strange and Fenella sat down on the edge of the bed while she tried to make some sense of what had happened. She knew that Sara's mother had been killed in a car accident while Sara was still a baby. She also knew how much her friend loved her father. According to Sara, he was the best father any child could possibly have and it was impossible to believe he would ever do anything to harm her. Yet Mr Parker had stood there and told Fenella he didn't have a daughter. More puzzling still, he had sounded as though he was telling the truth.

Perhaps he's had an accident too, Fenella thought. Perhaps he banged his head and lost his memory.

This was what had happened to Sebastian Snap after he had flown head first into a tree. He had thought he was a squirrel until he fell out of the nest he was trying to build and banged his head again. After that he had returned to normal.

Perhaps I ought to go down and hit Mr Parker on the head.

After a few moments' thought, Fenella decided to save this as a last resort because she didn't simply have Mr Parker's odd behaviour to worry about. Sara had blown the whistle, then she and Spot had disappeared. Fenella was positive that they must be in trouble and this was probably connected with the way Mr Parker had behaved. What she needed was advice. Igor was a human himself so he could probably help and Uncle Samuel certainly would. He was famous for being the wisest of all the vampires.

Fenella decided to fly back to her crypt, just in case Sara had gone there looking for her, and then go on to Blood Castle. On her way back she

63

flew very close to Mrs Potion's house, but Fenella was too preoccupied with the events of the night to have much interest in her surroundings. This was a shame. If she had looked down, she would surely have noticed the collection of statues that Mrs Potion had in her back garden.

Four

There was somebody or something in the crypt. Fenella swooped down low over the entrance, trying to identify the noise she could hear. It sounded as though huge quantities of water were gurgling down a plug and it brought a frown to Fenella's brow. She had had enough mysteries for one night.

'It can't be Sara,' she said to herself. 'She could never make a noise like that. Whoever it is had better have a good reason for being in my home. Otherwise it's going to be the worse for them.'

The moment Fenella entered the crypt and saw who her visitor was, her anger changed to surprise. There would be no reason to fly to Blood Castle to see Uncle Samuel because he was there, laying fast asleep in her coffin. The noise that had been bothering her was his snoring. With the coffin lid wide open, his snores were enough to shake the very walls of the crypt.

'Uncle Samuel,' Fenella said softly, tapping him on the shoulder. 'Wakey, wakey.'

Samuel merely snored a little louder. Now she thought of it, Fenella could remember Igor saying something about how it was becoming increasingly difficult to wake his master at night. When she tried a second time, Fenella raised her voice and tapped harder but this still had no effect – Samuel simply continued snoring. Before her third attempt, Fenella took a deep breath.

'UNCLE SAMUEL,' she bellowed, her mouth as close to his ear as she could get it. 'IT'S TIME TO WAKE UP.'

With a startled yelp, Samuel Suck sat bolt upright in the coffin, looking wildly around him. It was a moment or two before he recognized Fenella.

'There's no need to shout, dear,' he said severely. 'I'm not deaf.'

'I know, Uncle.'

Fenella was trying hard not to smile.

'Anyway, it was very nice of you to pop over to see me, my dear. You know you're always welcome at Blood Castle.'

'We're not at the castle, Uncle. You've come to visit me.'

'Have I really?' Now he looked around him, Samuel could see he wasn't in his own dungeon. 'No wonder I feel so tired.'

For the last two or three hundred years, Samuel hadn't done a great deal of flying. It was much easier to let people come to visit him.

'What did you come to see me about, Uncle?'

'Yes, I suppose there must be some reason for me being here.' As he had become older, Samuel had also become increasingly absent-minded. 'I wonder what it is.'

'It must be important for you to fly all this way.'

'I know,' Samuel shook his head in annoyance. 'It's a pity Igor isn't here. He'd be sure to—'

Samuel stopped in mid-sentence. He suddenly looked so sad that Fenella put out a hand to comfort him.

'What's the matter, Uncle?'

'I've just remembered.' Samuel's voice was shaky. 'It's Igor I wanted to talk to you about.'

'Is he all right? Nothing has happened to him, has it?'

For the moment Sara was forgotten. Fenella was too concerned about her uncle's servant.

'I think he's all right. He's been acting a bit strangely recently but that's nothing unusual for him. The thing is, he says he's going to leave Blood Castle and find a job somewhere else.'

'Leave Blood Castle? I don't believe it.' Fenella was appalled.

'Nor did I at first,' Samuel told her, 'but I'm afraid it's true. His mind is made up.'

'But why? Why in Drac's name would Igor want to go? It doesn't make sense.'

'It doesn't to me either. To be honest, dear, I don't know what I'll do without him. Igor has been the best servant any vampire could possibly wish for.'

Samuel said this with a sniff. Igor had been far more than a servant to him. He had also been a friend.

'But why?' Fenella repeated. 'There has to be a reason.'

'Oh there is, dear. I think it's something to do with Geronimo.'

'Aren't you sure?'

'Not really. Igor did start to explain but I was so upset I began shouting at the poor fellow. After that Igor wouldn't say anything. You know how stubborn he can be.'

Now Samuel was sounding ashamed of himself. He looked so unhappy sitting there in the coffin that Fenella leaned forward to nuzzle his neck.

'Is there anything I can do to help, Uncle?'

'I don't know, my dear. I thought perhaps you might fly over to the castle and have a few words with Igor. The two of you have always got on well together.'

'Of course I will.' Fenella was sure she could soon persuade Igor to change his mind. 'Are you going to fly back with me?'

'I will if you don't mind waiting a little before we set out. I'd quite forgotten what a long journey it was to get here.'

Looking at her uncle, Fenella could see just how tired he was. Even with her to help him, she didn't think it was a good idea for Samuel to attempt the return journey so soon.

'Why don't you stay here until tomorrow night and fly back then,' she suggested. 'I can always use the spare coffin at the castle.'

'Are you sure you don't mind?'

The suggestion appeared to cheer Samuel up a little.

'Of course I don't,' Fenella told him. 'Besides, that way I shall have more time to work on Igor. Everything should be sorted out before you get home.'

'I do hope so, dear.'

Poor Samuel sounded so sad and forlorn that Fenella had to turn away so he wouldn't see the green tears glistening in her eyes.

'Igor has to stay,' she said fiercely to herself. 'He has to. I won't let him leave.'

For the moment, all thoughts of Sara had completely gone from her mind.

Igor didn't have a suitcase but after a lot of hunting around he did manage to find the brown paper bag he used to wear as a child. Even when he had found it, there wasn't anything for him to put inside. The only clothes he owned were the ones he had been wearing for as long as he could remember and he could slip his pet beetles into a pocket.

I know, he thought, yawning hugely. I'll make myself some sandwiches to eat on the journey. I can put them into the bag.

The trouble was, he felt so tired. Even with matchsticks to keep his eyes open, he kept nodding off and banging his head on the kitchen table. It took him so long to make the sandwiches that he was feeling really hungry by the time they were ready. Before he knew it, they were all gone. Apart from a few crumbs, he still didn't have anything to put in his bag.

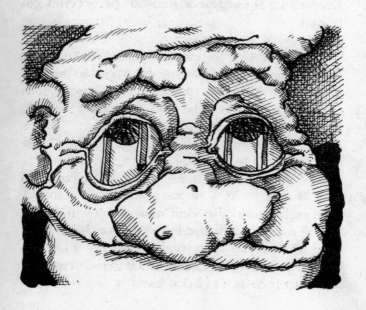

Perhaps I ought to start wearing it again ... Igor was feeling sorry for himself ... I might have to if I'm leaving Blood Castle.

He was still sitting at the table in the Great Hall, wondering about what to put in the bag in between nodding off and banging his head on the table, when Fenella came rushing in.

'What's all this rubbish I've heard about you leaving, Igor?' she demanded. 'Tell me it isn't true.'

'But it is true, Miss Fenella. I've been doing my packing.'

As he spoke, Igor hung his head in shame. It was almost as bad having to upset Miss Fenella as it had been upsetting the Master. It made him feel as though he was letting them down.

Fenella didn't answer him immediately. She went to sit at the other end of the table instead. Until now she hadn't realized just how serious the problem was. She had been sure Uncle Samuel must be mistaken.

'I thought you were fond of the Master,' she said at last.

'I am, Mistress. I am. He's been like a father to me.'

'You do like it at Blood Castle, don't you?'

'It's my home, Miss Fenella. I've lived here most of my life.'

'In that case, why let some silly ghost drive you out? Surely he can't be that bad.'

'He isn't,' Igor said darkly. 'He's worse. He's killing me.'

'What do you mean?'

'He won't let me sleep, Mistress. I haven't had a wink since he arrived and I can't carry on much longer. I don't want to leave but I've got to.'

Once Igor had started, it all came pouring out. He had lived with vampires so long that in some ways he behaved like one. Night time was when Samuel was up and about and this was when he needed his servant. So Igor stayed up all night too and didn't go to bed until the morning when Samuel was safely tucked away in his coffin.

'I don't see what the problem is, Igor.' Fenella was more puzzled than ever. 'Ghosts are night-time creatures too.'

'This Grottimo isn't, Miss Fenella. He rests all night just so he can keep me awake all day.'

'What does he do?'

'He haunts me, Mistress, that's what he does. He dances round my bed waving that dratted tomahawk of his and whooping and hollering all day long.'

'Every day?'

'Every day,' Igor told her. 'If I don't get some sleep soon, I don't know what I'll do. I keep dozing off at night and that isn't safe. What happens when one of the Master's inventions goes wrong and I'm not there to help him? I'd never forgive myself if anything happened to him. It's far better if the Master gets himself another servant.'

For a moment Fenella simply looked at the miserable Igor. Then she rose to her feet.

'Twaddle,' she said. 'Absolute bunkum. You know it and so do I. Uncle Samuel wants *you* to be his servant, not anybody else.'

'But I have to sleep, Mistress. If I don't, I'll end up a ghost like Gerrymouse or whatever his name is.'

'You can get some sleep now. Uncle won't be back until tomorrow. Meanwhile I'm going to have a word with our ghostly friend. Where will I find him?'

'He'll be floating around somewhere, Miss Fenella. He seems to like that cupboard where you first saw him.'

'I'll find him wherever he is. You go to sleep now and leave everything to me.'

Fenella was talking to herself. Igor had already slipped the matchsticks out from under his eyelids and was sleeping peacefully with his head resting on the table.

As Igor had said, Geronimo was in the cupboard in the turret room. He was hovering there, just above the ground, with his eyes tightly closed. Fenella wondered exactly what he was doing because she knew that ghosts never slept. She also knew that ghosts came out at night, just like vampires. Perhaps there was something special about Red Indian ghosts.

'Geronimo,' she said sharply.

The ghost's eyes snapped open at once. As soon as he saw who his visitor was, his face split into a broad smile.

'Hello, Fenella,' he said. 'It's good to see you again.'

'I'm not sure whether it's good to see you or not. Come out here. I want to talk to you.'

Geronimo did as he was told, floating to the middle of the room while Fenella sat on a chair.

'What is it?' he enquired.

'I want to know what you've been doing to Igor.'

'Me?' the ghost's face was innocence itself. 'I haven't been doing anything.'

'Oh yes you have. You've been haunting him.'

'That's what ghosts are supposed to do,' Geronimo pointed out. 'Anyway, it doesn't matter. Old Iggy isn't a bit afraid of me.'

'Maybe not, but poor Igor isn't getting any sleep. You've got to stop.'

'I can't.'

Geronimo was shaking his head.

'Of course you can,' Fenella said impatiently.

'But I can't, Fenella. If there's a human in the same house as me and he's asleep, I have to haunt him. I couldn't stop myself if I tried. It's all right when Iggy is awake – then I can talk to him the same way I'm talking to you. But if he's asleep, I don't have any choice.'

'That's a nuisance.'

Fenella knew that all ghosts were different and that there were certain things that were beyond their control. However, there was one thing she didn't understand.

'Ghosts haunt at night,' she said.

'Not Red Indian ghosts,' Geronimo answered. 'We only come out during the day.'

'Why is that?'

'We don't like the dark.' Geronimo was looking

embarrassed. 'It's full of evil spirits.'

'You're a spirit yourself.' Fenella couldn't believe her ears. 'I've never ever heard anything so ridiculous.'

'That's what everybody says,' Geronimo told her sadly, 'but it's true. You can ask Long Nose or Prickly Hedgehog or any of the others and they'll tell you the same. All of us Red Indian ghosts can only haunt during the day.'

So far Fenella didn't feel as though she was doing very well. It seemed that Red Indian ghosts had almost as many strange habits as humans.

'Did you know that Igor was thinking of leaving Blood Castle?' she asked.

'Why would he want to do that?'

'Because of you, Geronimo. Humans need to sleep, and Igor hasn't been able to sleep since you arrived. He can't stand any more. It's making him ill.'

'I didn't realize that.' Geronimo's voice was suddenly very small. 'That makes me feel really bad. I'm quite fond of old Iggy.'

'That isn't what Igor thinks,' Fenella told him. 'He thinks you're doing it on purpose.'

Neither of them spoke for a few moments. Then Geronimo's face brightened.

'Hey,' he said. 'I've had an idea. Why doesn't Iggy sleep at night while I'm keeping out of the way of evil spirits. Then there won't be any problem.'

'He can't. That's when Igor is working for Uncle Samuel.'

'I hadn't thought of that. It seems that both Iggy and me are stuck.'

'Except for one thing,' Fenella pointed out. 'Igor has lived here most of his life. What's more, Uncle Samuel needs him.'

For a long moment Geronimo simply stared at Fenella. Then he slowly nodded his head.

'What you really mean is that this isn't my home and nobody needs me.'

'You said it, not me.' Fenella told him. 'You're entitled to stay here as long as you like. You know the laws of vampiredom.'

'And you know I couldn't drive poor old Iggy out. I'm the one who ought to do the leaving. It's a shame, though. I liked Blood Castle from the first moment I saw it. After all those horrid skyscrapers in New York, it looked like somewhere I could call home.'

'Nobody is telling you to leave.' Fenella was beginning to feel mean.

'But it would be easier if I left, wouldn't it?'

'Yes, I suppose it would.'

'In that case, I'd better be saying goodbye. Give my best to Samuel and thank him for his hospitality.'

As Geronimo started drifting towards the wall, Fenella felt worse than ever. Although she knew there was no other answer, she could see how upset the ghost was. It was a pity her friend

George wasn't around. He was a ghost too and he could probably have given some useful advice. But he wasn't there and—

'Wait a minute, Geronimo.'

The idea had come to her like a bolt from the blue. Thinking about George had reminded Fenella of something he had once told her. It might just be the solution to their problem.

'What is it, Fenella?'

Geronimo had stopped by the wall and turned to face her.

'I might have thought of a way both you and Igor could stay.' Her idea was seeming better by the moment. 'How would you feel about going to see a wizard?'

'A wizard? I thought they were all gone. Didn't they all become younger and younger until they eventually faded away.'

'All except one. He managed to make some magic to stop himself getting any younger.'

'Big deal.' Geronimo didn't sound very impressed. 'How does that help me.'

'I could take you to see him. We'd ask him to make some magic for you, give you some kind of potion that turned you into a proper night-time ghost. Then there wouldn't be any problem. Igor could get his sleep during the day and you wouldn't have to leave. What do you think?'

'I think it's a marvellous idea.' Geronimo was

all smiles. 'When do we go to see this wizard of yours?'

'How about now?' Fenella suggested.

'Let's get going then.'

'I've just got one or two things to collect first.'

'Okey-dokey. While you're doing that, I'll go and break the good news to Iggy.'

'Fine.'

As they might not be back to the castle before daylight, Fenella wanted to make sure she had some cream and goggles with her. She knew Uncle Samuel wouldn't mind if she borrowed his. She was halfway down the stairs to the dungeon when she realized that what Geronimo had said he was going to do wasn't fine at all. However, it was already too late for her to do anything.

'THAT DRATTED GHOST HAS WOKEN ME UP AGAIN.' Although Igor was in the Great Hall, his outraged bellow carried clearly to where Fenella was standing. 'IT'S JUST NOT FAIR. NOW HE'S HAUNTING ME AT NIGHT TOO.'

With a little groan, Fenella started back up the stairs. She really did hope the Wizard Yu-u-uck would be able to do something to help.

Five

'The cave doesn't look at all the way George described it to me,' Fenella said doubtfully.

For a moment or two she wondered whether she had come to the wrong place but then she shook her head. She was positive that George had told her the wizard lived on the slopes of Snowdon, the highest mountain in Wales, and this was where she had flown with Geronimo. Besides, the cave was exactly where she had expected it to be. The trouble was, it looked like an ordinary cave. There was nothing to indicate that a wizard lived there.

'What's happened to the purple flashes George talked about?' Fenella's voice was still doubtful. 'And the rumbles like thunder?'

'Perhaps your friend was exaggerating,' Geronimo suggested. 'Ghosts do that sometimes.'

'Perhaps,' Fenella agreed. 'Let's go and take a look.'

As they drew nearer, they could hear strange

noises coming from inside the cave. However, they didn't sound at all like thunder. Somebody was screaming as though he was in pain.

'What can be happening?' Fenella wondered, hurrying forward.

'It reminds me of my grandfather, Big Chief Bad Shot,' Geronimo told her. 'He used to make noises like that whenever he shot an arrow through his foot.'

'Wizards don't have arrows,' Fenella pointed out.

By now they were close enough to see inside the cave. Everything appeared to be in the most dreadful mess. Tables and chairs and large pots were scattered around all over the floor, mixed with pieces of broken plates and cups.

'Are all wizards this untidy?' Geronimo asked.

'I don't know,' Fenella answered. 'I've never met one before.'

It didn't seem as though she was about to meet one now. The only person in the cave was a skinny, old man in a nightshirt. He also had a long, straggly beard which was tied around his waist to stop it from dragging on the floor. The beard was bright green and so was the hair which stuck straight up from his head. It was this strange figure who was doing the screaming, both hands clutching his bottom as he pranced around at the back of the cave.

'What in Drac's name is he doing?' Fenella was beginning to think she had made a serious mistake.

'It's probably the Wizard's War Dance,' Geronimo said helpfully. 'Either that or he's trying to make it rain.'

'Don't be so silly,' Fenella told him.

Still screaming, the man had stopped holding his bottom. Now he was clutching his stomach, doubled over while he staggered around the cave. He was obviously suffering a great deal.

'It looks like a dance to me.'

Fenella was too fascinated by the weird performance to pay any attention to Geronimo. It ended abruptly when the man pranced head first into the wall of the cave. After that he sat down on the floor with a bump, his eyes tightly closed. For the time being at least, he had stopped screaming.

'Do you think we ought to clap?' Geronimo asked.

'I think you ought to be quiet. Excuse me, sir,' she went on, speaking to the man on the floor. 'I was wondering whether you could help me.'

'I can't even help myself,' the man on the floor answered in a surprisingly deep voice, his eyes still closed. 'Go away, whoever you are. Clear off and leave me in peace.'

'It is important,' Fenella persisted.

This time the man did open his eyes. When he saw Fenella, he groaned.

'Jumping jellybeans,' he moaned. 'A vampire is just what I needed. Go ahead then. Suck all the blood out of me. See if I care.'

The very thought made Fenella shudder.

'All I wanted to know was where I can find the Wizard Yu-u-uck.'

'I ... OUCH! OOOWWW! OOOHHH!'

He didn't finish because he was up and prancing again, hopping on one leg this time while he held the other. However, he only did this for a few moments. Then he hopped high in the air, performed a double somersault and dived head first into a large cauldron. There he stayed, his skinny white legs kicking feebly in the air.

'That's brilliant,' Geronimo said admiringly. 'He's an acrobat as well.'

'Are all ghosts that stupid?' a voice asked.

The unexpected interruption made Fenella look up sharply. When she had first entered the cave, she had noticed the large white cat sitting on a shelf; but it was only now she paid any real attention to it.

'You spoke,' she said in amazement.

'How very observant of you,' the cat replied. 'Vampires are obviously highly intelligent creatures as well.'

'You must be the wizard's cat.'

'That's right.' The cat stood up and stretched. 'Yucky and me go back years.'

'In that case you can probably help me. I came here to see the Wizard Yu-u-uck.'

'You already have.'

'What do you mean?' Fenella didn't understand immediately.

'Those scrawny, white shanks waving at us from the cauldron,' the cat explained. 'They belong to the great, all-powerful Wizard Yu-u-uck.'

'He doesn't look great and all-powerful to me,' Geronimo commented. 'What's happened to him?'

'Why don't you ask him?' the cat suggested.

'The morning session should be over by now. Are you ready to come out yet, Yucky old mate?'

'Of course I am.' The wizard's voice was muffled by the cauldron. 'Is somebody going to help me?'

He looked even less like a great and all-powerful wizard once Fenella went to his assistance. The cauldron obviously hadn't been washed recently and there was brown goo stuck to his hair and beard. As she looked at him, Fenella was convinced that coming to Snowdon had been a complete waste of time.

The wizard told Fenella and Geronimo everything. He told them about his wife Griselda, and how she loved practical jokes. He explained how he had lost his temper and turned her into a toad. He said how she had plotted her revenge for seven hundred years until a Prince had finally released her from the spell.

'But what has she done?' Fenella asked. 'I always thought a wizard's magic was much more powerful than a witch's.'

'It is,' Yu-u-uck agreed gloomily. 'At least, it is as long as the wizard has his spellbook. That's where all my power is, you see, in my spellbook, and I don't have it any more. Without it, I'm helpless. Grisly knew that, of course. That's why she sneaked in and stole it while I was out.'

'Isn't that a bit careless?' Geronimo asked.

'Leaving the spellbook lying around when it's so valuable.'

'Grisly was the only one who could do it,' Yu-u-uck explained, sounding more gloomy than ever. 'There's a spell on the cave entrance while I'm out to stop anybody coming inside. Unfortunately, Grisly was my wife so it didn't affect her. It's the same with the spellbook. Nobody else would even be able to touch it but Grisly needed to move it when she was doing the dusting and things. I made a special spell for her so she could pick it up safely. The trouble is, I forgot to remove the spell after I'd turned her into a toad. As I wasn't likely to be seeing her any more, I didn't think it was necessary.'

'Are you saying Griselda can use all your magic as well as her own now she has the spellbook?' Fenella was becoming quite interested in the story.

'Oh no.' Yu-u-uck seemed shocked at the idea. 'Grisly can't even open it. What she's done is remove all my power. That means she can use her magic on me. I can still do a few very simple spells but not enough to protect myself.'

'You can't do a spell to make me haunt at night instead of during the day, can you?' Geronimo asked hopefully.

The wizard shook his head.

'That's far too complicated to do without my spellbook.'

'Yucky can't even feed us properly,' the cat said. 'He keeps magicking up food in tins and he then can't manage the tin-opening spell.'

'I do wish you wouldn't keep calling me Yucky,' Yu-u-uck said irritably.

'I'm sorry, Yucky old mate,' the cat replied, winking at Fenella. 'I can't get out of the habit. Anyway, shouldn't you be getting yourself ready? Grisly will be starting up again soon.'

'Oh yes. Thanks for reminding me.'

The wizard rushed over to a pile of junk in the corner of the cave and started sorting frantically through it. When he found the battered red motorcycle helmet, he grunted with satisfaction and began strapping it on his head. Fenella watched this with amazement. She expected

wizards to wear cloaks and pointed hats, not nightshirts and helmets. The green hair and beard were something of a shock as well, although she assumed they must be one of Griselda's practical jokes.

'What's the helmet for?' she enquired.

'It's almost time for Yucky's flying lessons,' the cat explained.

'Flying lessons?' Fenella repeated blankly.

'That's right. It's the same every morning. First we have the pin-sticking, then we have—'

'Wait a moment,' Fenella interrupted. 'What's the pin-sticking?'

'It's quite simple,' the cat said. 'Yucky's charming lady wife has made a wax model of him. Every morning when she gets up, she sticks pins into it. Wherever she sticks a pin in the model, that's where poor old Yucky hurts. Today it was his bottom, tummy and leg. Tomorrow it will probably be his head, back and arms.'

'How terrible.' Fenella was shocked. 'I think that's awful.'

'Yucky's not too keen on it himself,' the cat pointed out. 'Anyway when she's fed up with sticking in pins, Grisly goes off to have her breakfast. The flying lessons start straight after she's finished.'

Fenella looked across at the wizard. Now he had the helmet in place, he was busy strapping padding to his arms and legs.

'Exactly what are these flying lessons?' she asked.

'Oh, Yucky zooms around a lot, a bit like a model aeroplane. Anyway, I must be off outside.' The cat jumped down from the shelf. 'If I were you, I'd do the same.'

'Why?'

'It's not very safe in here with Yucky shooting around like a demented rocket, bouncing off the walls and ceilings and things. Mind you, the worst days are when poor old Yucky is frozen to the spot while all the furniture flies around. I can tell you, he really needs his helmet then.'

The cat was already walking towards the entrance and Fenella and Geronimo quickly followed. The cave definitely didn't sound like a safe place to be.

The banging and crashing and yelling seemed to go on for a long time. When it eventually finished, the cat continued washing his paw for a few moments before he looked up at Fenella.

'It should be safe to go inside now,' he said.

'Are you sure?'

'Oh yes. Grisly will be off to do her shopping now. Yucky should be safe until she's had her lunch. That's the worst time of all because Yucky never quite knows what to expect then. It all depends what kind of mood Grisly is in.'

The three of them went back inside the cave.

Although the furniture was still scattered all over the floor, there was no sign of the wizard. Geronimo looked in the cauldrons while Fenella poked around under a pile of chairs. Neither of them met with any success.

'This is something new.' The cat sounded concerned. 'Where are you, Yucky old mate?'

'If you called me by my proper name, I might tell you.'

The wizard's voice came from above and they all looked up. Yu-u-uck's helmet was touching the ceiling while the rest of him dangled helplessly below, the nightshirt billowing around his legs.

'Do all wizards wear red and green striped underpants?' Geronimo asked interestedly.

'Be quiet,' Fenella hissed. 'Is there anything I can do, Wizard Yu-u-uck?'

'No, not unless you know any magic,' Yu-u-uck answered gloomily. 'I'm stuck here until my wife decides to let me down. I suppose I'll get used to it after a while.'

'Only your helmet is stuck,' the cat said, 'Take that off and you should be able to come down.'

'That's absolutely brilliant, you feline fool,' the wizard snarled. 'If I drop down from this height, I'll break both my legs.'

'It's all right,' Fenella said. 'I can stand underneath and catch you.'

'Are vampires any good at catching?' Yu-u-uck

asked suspiciously.

'It's one of the things we do best.'

'All right, then. I suppose I'd better risk it. Even if you do drop me, a couple of broken legs can't be any worse than what Grisly has in store for me.'

It took Yu-u-uck a while to undo the strap but when he did drop, Fenella caught him, just as she had promised. Although the wizard was very pleased about not breaking his legs, he wasn't quite so happy when the helmet came unstuck a moment later, falling to bounce off the top of his head. Some of the words he used while he was rubbing his head were quite rude.

'Yucky, really,' the cat said. 'I'm ashamed of you.'

'Just you wait until Grisly gets around to you,' the wizard retorted. 'Then we'll see what you have to say.'

'Do you think she will do something to me?' The cat sounded uneasy.

'She's bound to.' For the first time since Fenella's arrival, Yu-u-uck was almost smiling. 'Sooner or later she'll remember how much she didn't like you.'

'Is it as bad as this every day?' Geronimo asked the wizard.

'Oh no. Some days it's much worse. Grisly must have been in a hurry today.'

'How long do you think it will last?'

'That's difficult to say. Grisly was a toad for seven centuries. Knowing her, I'd say it will be at least a thousand years before she decides she's got her own back.'

'How terrible.' Fenella was appalled. 'Isn't there anything you can do?'

'I only wish there was.' Yu-u-uck sounded gloomier than ever. 'For a start, I can't even get out of the cave. She's cast a spell to stop me leaving. And even if I could leave, it wouldn't do me any good. I wouldn't know where to find her or the spellbook.'

'Don't you have any ideas?'

'None at all. The only time I've seen her since she stole the spellbook, she told me she had a nice, new home but I don't know where. All Grisly said was that she was going to live among humans.'

'Why would she want to do that?' Fenella couldn't imagine anything worse.

'Well, she never did like humans very much. Now she's stopped being a toad, she likes them even less. Apparently they did all manner of nasty things to her while she was under my spell. She wants to be revenged on them almost as much as she wants to be revenged on me. That's why she wants to live among them – it will make it easier for her to get up to all kinds of mischief. Grisly even said she's taken a human name, Mrs Potion or something.'

'What did you say?'

Ever since Uncle Samuel had told her about Igor's problems, Fenella had hardly spared a thought for Sara. Mention of Griselda's new name brought it all flooding back to her. Mrs Potion was the name of the woman who had moved into a house on Sara's road. If Mrs Potion was really Griselda, Sara had had every reason to be frightened of her. Fenella now knew that something truly dreadful must have happened to her friend. She could even think of the reason Sara's father had denied having a daughter – Griselda must have put a forgetting spell on him.

'She said her new name was Mrs Potion,' Yu-u-uck repeated. 'I'm sure that's the name Grisly mentioned.'

'In that case,' Fenella said slowly, 'I think I might know where your wife is living.'

For a moment, Yu-u-uck's expression brightened. Then his face fell again.

'Even if you're right,' he said, 'I'm afraid it doesn't do me any good. There's no way I can get to the spellbook while I'm stuck here in the cave. I've already tried getting out and it's no good. What magic I have left simply isn't strong enough. Unfortunately, Grisly knew exactly what she was doing.'

'Perhaps I could get the spellbook for you,' Fenella suggested.

'Could you really?' The wizard had suddenly

cheered up again.

'I can't think why not,' Fenella told him.

'I can,' Geronimo said. 'You're forgetting something, Fenella.'

'That's right,' the cat agreed. 'Nobody except Yucky and Grisly can touch the spellbook.'

'Oh dear.' Now it was Fenella's turn to be upset. 'I'd forgotten that.'

'It might not be too much of a problem.' Unlike Fenella, Yu-u-uck was still cheerful. 'Touching spells are quite easy. I should have enough magic left to manage that. The question is, are you really prepared to fetch the spellbook for me? It may be dangerous.'

'I'll go,' Fenella said firmly.

She knew she had to. It was no longer simply a matter of helping Uncle Samuel and Igor. Sara had to be rescued from whatever plight she was in.

'If you're successful, I'll be more grateful than you can possibly imagine.' Yu-u-uck's voice was trembling with emotion, and he obviously meant every word. 'You can have anything you want. All my magic will be at your disposal whenever you need it.'

'We can sort that out later,' Fenella said impatiently. 'Just get on with your touching spell.'

'I will, I will.' The wizard had already bustled to the back of the cave and was rummaging around in the furniture for a cauldron. 'It won't take a jiffy.'

'While you're about it, can you include a human friend of mine in the spell? I may need his help.'

'That's no problem. Once the spell is prepared, I can make it for as many people as I like.'

Yu-u-uck actually seemed quite happy as he set to work, whistling cheerily between his teeth. Fenella only hoped she could actually manage to do what she had promised.

'Fenella,' Geronimo said quietly. 'Do you mind if I ask you a question?'

'Of course not.'

'Well, what I want to know is, does a witch's magic work on vampires?'

'Yes, it does.'

'So this Grisly Potion or whatever her name is could do something horrible to you if you were caught?'

'Yes, I suppose she could.'

This wasn't something Fenella particularly wanted to think about.

'Aren't you frightened?'

'I'm terrified.'

It was an entirely new experience for Fenella because there weren't very many things which were dangerous to vampires. For a few seconds Geronimo didn't speak.

'I'm not worth it,' he said at last. 'Forget about

the spellbook, Fenella. It's much easier if I simply leave Blood Castle. I'd much rather do that than have anything nasty happen to you.'

'Thank you, Geronimo.' Irritating as he was at times, Fenella was becoming quite fond of the ghost. 'That's a lovely thing for you to say but I really do have to go, however dangerous it is. I'm not just doing it for you and Uncle and Igor. A friend of mine is in terrible danger.'

Fenella was hoping that she wasn't already too late.

Six

As soon as he saw the black dot in the distance, Igor left the battlements and wearily started lurching down the spiral staircase. Going up was easy for him because his short leg was on the inside of the bend but going down was much more of a problem, even when he wasn't so tired. He had collected several bruises from where he had banged into the wall long before he reached the Great Hall.

'Miss Fenella is coming, Master,' Igor announced breathlessly.

'Excellent. Go up and tell her I'm waiting for her.'

Fenella had already set off for Griselda's house when Samuel returned to Blood Castle. However, Igor and Geronimo had given him the details of what had been happening while he was away. What he had heard had made Samuel most concerned about Fenella's safety and he was relieved to know she was on her way back. At least the witch hadn't turned her into a human or anything terrible like that.

By the time poor Igor had run back up to the battlements, he was almost dropping with exhaustion. He was also completely out of breath. Although he tried to say hello to Fenella, all he could do was pant.

'For Drac's sake, Igor,' Fenella snapped impatiently. 'I'm not in the mood for your little games tonight. If you've got anything to say, just spit it out.'

When Igor tried again, he still didn't do any better as his breath was coming in great sobbing gasps which made speech impossible. The best he could manage was a hideous leer which was the closest he could come to a friendly smile.

'I sometimes wonder about you,' Fenella said irritably. 'Can you at least tell me if Uncle Samuel is back?'

This time Igor didn't attempt to speak. He simply nodded his head, showering Fenella with a great cloud of dandruff.

'Well, at least that's something. Come on, Igor. Don't just stand there.'

Fenella started off down the stairs, pushing Igor ahead of her. Vampires can walk very fast when they want to and Fenella was in a hurry. This meant Igor had to go very fast as well, bouncing from wall to wall, and by the time they reached the Great Hall he was exhausted. What with not getting any sleep and whizzing up and down spiral staircases, he was so tired he had to hang on to the door to stop himself from collapsing. However, nobody was paying any attention to him. It was Fenella that Samuel was concerned about. As soon as he saw her, he leapt out of his chair.

'Are you all right, dear?' he enquired anxiously.

'I'm fine, thank you.'

Fenella affectionately nuzzled her uncle's neck before she sank down into a chair.

'Are you sure, dear. You look absolutely exhausted.'

'So am I,' Igor wanted to shout but he still didn't have enough breath.

'I am rather tired, Uncle,' Fenella admitted. 'I've done a lot of flying the last two nights and I was up all day yesterday.'

'You poor thing,' Samuel said sympathetically. 'Don't just loll around there, Igor. Go and get Fenella something to eat and drink.'

Igor nodded wearily, releasing another cloud of dandruff, and started off for the kitchen. After a few steps he decided that walking was too much of an effort and dropped to his hands and knees to crawl instead. There were definitely occasions when he was sure that there must be better jobs than working for a vampire.

Samuel and Fenella had agreed that there would

be no discussion of the night's events until after Igor had returned. But Igor didn't return. They waited and waited but still there was no sign of him.

'Wote cun hay bay doving?' Samuel said impatiently. 'Hay hairs boon heehovung must strainly roosently.'

'Teeth, Uncle,' Fenella reminded him.

'Slurry, dire.'

Samuel reached into his mouth and removed the false teeth he had put in ready for the expected refreshments. Lying on the table they looked like one of the steel traps gamekeepers used to set to catch poachers. Although they were superb for eating with, Samuel couldn't speak properly when he was wearing them.

'That's better,' he said, giving his gums a lick. 'I was just wondering what young Igor could be doing. He really has been acting most strangely recently.'

'He is very tired, Uncle. Perhaps I ought to go and check that he's all right.'

'No, I'll go, dear. You stay here and rest.'

When Samuel first reached the kitchen, he wasn't sure what Igor was doing. All he could see of his servant was his bottom and legs because the top half of Igor was completely hidden inside the oven. For a moment Samuel simply stared in amazement. Then he realized what Igor must be doing and stepped forward angrily to kick him on the bottom.

'Ouch,' Igor yelped as his head hit the back of the oven. 'That hurt.'

He had been getting the maggot pasties out of the oven when he had fallen asleep. It had been so warm and comfortable he simply hadn't been able to keep his eyes open any longer.

'It serves you right,' Samuel said unsympathetically. 'Fancy practising one of your silly games of hide and seek when you should have been getting something for Fenella to eat.'

'But, Master,' Igor protested. 'I wasn't—'

'I don't want any "buts", Igor. You should be ashamed of yourself. No wonder you're blushing.'

'I'm not blushing, Master.' Igor had just realized how hot his head felt. 'The oven was still on.'

'I've waited long enough.' Samuel wasn't paying any attention to him. 'Get a move on or there's going to be trouble.'

'But, Master—'

Igor didn't have a chance to explain because the old vampire was already stamping out of the kitchen.

'It's all right, dear,' he told Fenella when he was back in the Great Hall. 'I've had words with Igor. He should be here in a moment.'

It wasn't very long before they heard Igor coming. At least, they assumed it was Igor. Instead of the normal uneven slip-slap of his feet against the flagstones there was a strange scraping sound. It was as though something was being dragged along the floor.

'What's he up to now?' Samuel demanded.

As the two vampires watched in astonishment, the tray containing the pasties and the glasses of HBS were pushed through the doorway. The tray was followed by Igor who was crawling on his stomach, his eyes half closed.

'Is this some silly new game, Igor. Stand up and carry the tray properly.'

'I daren't, Master. I keep falling asleep and I

don't want to drop it.'

'Here. Let me do it.'

Fenella quickly rose from her seat and went across to collect the tray. Then she went back to pick up Igor. As soon as he was seated in a chair, Igor's head fell forward on his chest and his eyes closed.

'Stay awake, Igor,' Fenella said, slapping him gently on the cheek. 'What I have to say is important.'

'I am list—'

Igor's head fell forward again and he began snoring. Fenella slapped him on the cheek a second time.

'Come on, Igor. You must listen. This concerns you.'

'I will, Mistress.'

Igor's eyes were closing again before he had finished speaking. This time Fenella had to shake him.

'I can't get the spellbook, Igor,' she said urgently. 'You'll have to do it. You'll have to break into the witch's house and steal back the spellbook.'

'What did you say?' Suddenly Igor was wide awake. He had never felt less like sleeping. 'Was I dreaming, Mistress, or did I hear you say something about breaking into the witch's house?'

'You weren't dreaming, Igor.'

Igor's face had still been very red from where he had cooked it in the oven. Now it had gone very pale. Although his mouth opened once or twice, no sounds came out. It made him look like a very ugly goldfish.

'What happened, dear?" Samuel enquired. 'I guessed that something must have gone wrong.'

'I couldn't get near to the house,' Fenella explained. 'There's some kind of anti-vampire barrier all round it and it was like flying into a brick wall. And I couldn't get any closer no matter how high up I flew. Griselda must have known I was coming.'

'What makes you so sure it's a vampire barrier, dear?'

'I saw a human walking past along the road. He didn't have any trouble at all but when I went down to the ground I still hit an invisible wall. Vampires just can't get close to Griselda's house.'

'I see,' Samuel thoughtfully. 'I wonder why the witch thought she had to protect herself against vampires.'

'I was wondering that too, Master.'

Igor was wondering a lot of things. This was why he was still wide awake.

'It was probably when Heinz Beans used the whistle,' Fenella said. 'Griselda must have seen it and recognized what it was.'

'I suppose so but that doesn't help us with our other problem. We still don't have any idea what the witch might have done to Sara.'

'Whatever it is, the spellbook is the only hope we have of rescuing her. Once Yu-u-uck has it back his magic will be much stronger than Griselda's. He should be able to undo any mischief she's done. Like I said, as I can't get near the house, Igor will have to fetch the spellbook for us.'

'Me, Mistress?'

It was the moment Igor had been dreading. This Griselda sounded as though she was really dangerous.

'I'm afraid so,' Fenella told him. 'You're the only person apart from me who can do it. I'll fly you as close to Griselda's house as I can. Then you can go in and steal the spellbook.'

'I can't, Mistress.'

'What?' Samuel couldn't believe his ears. 'Are you saying you won't do anything to help Sara?'

'I can't, Master,' Igor repeated miserably.

'I'm surprised at you, Igor.' There was disgust in Samuel's voice. 'I know the witch must frighten you but I didn't think that would stop you from trying to help Sara.'

'I am frightened, Master,' Igor admitted. 'I don't want to be turned into a butterfly or a policeman or anything nasty like that – but that isn't what's stopping me. I'd still go if I could, but I can't.'

'In Drac's name, why not?'

'Well, Master, if this witch has put up a vampire barrier she's hardly likely to leave the door unlocked or a window open. I'm not very good at things like that. I'd never be able to break into the house without the witch hearing me.'

'That's easily solved, Igor.' Samuel was all smiles again. 'You'll just have to wait until Griselda goes out.'

'No, Uncle,' Fenella told him. 'I don't think that will work. Griselda will be like Yu-u-uck. She'll put a spell on the house whenever she goes out. Igor would have to break into the house while she was there.'

All three of them fell silent. Although none of them even considered giving up, there didn't seem to be any solution to their problem.

'Geronimo,' Samuel said suddenly. 'He could just drift in through the walls. The witch would never hear him.'

'That's a brilliant idea, Master.'

'I'm afraid it isn't, Uncle.' Fenella was shaking her head. 'He's a ghost. Geronimo would never be able to pick up the spellbook.'

'I'm sorry, dear. I'd forgotten.'

Ghostly hands weren't much use for picking up things.

'It's a shame we don't know where that Big Bundle is,' Samuel went on after a pause.

'Do you mean Bert Bungle, Uncle?' For an

instant Fenella hadn't known who Samuel was talking about. But of course he meant Bert, her burglar 'friend'.

'That's the chappy. I seem to remember he was very good with locks and things.'

'He was, Uncle, but I wouldn't have any idea where to find him.'

'I would, Mistress,' Igor broke in excitedly. 'He's on a lighthouse.'

Both Fenella and Samuel looked at Igor in amazement.

'What are you talking about, Igor?' Samuel demanded.

'I saw his photograph in the newspaper, Master.'

'But you can't read, Igor. What were you doing with a newspaper?'

'My fish and chips were wrapped in it, Master.' Igor was beginning to dribble. He always did this when he was excited. 'I think I've still got it somewhere.'

Igor scurried off. A few moments later he returned, waving a crumpled piece of greasy newspaper in his hand. Although it wasn't a very good photograph and there were several bits of stale chip stuck to it, Fenella and Samuel could see that Igor was right. The man in the picture was unmistakably Bert Bungle and he was definitely standing on a lighthouse. Once Igor had licked away some of the scraps of fish and

chips, Fenella could read what was written underneath the photograph. It said THE NEW KEEPER OF THE BALLYSTONE LIGHT, MR BERT BUNGLE. Better still, both Fenella and Samuel knew exactly where Ballystone was. Vampires had an excellent sense of direction but lighthouses could still be useful to them on very dark nights.

'Right,' Fenella said, rising to her feet. 'You'd better go and get some sleep, Igor. You'll have a busy night tomorrow. While you do that I'm going to pay a visit to Mr Bert Bungle.'

She was sure he would be delighted to meet her again.

* * *

Once upon a time Bert Bungle had been a burglar and he had been quite happy. Stealing suited him much better than working and he hadn't had any worries in the world. Then he had met the vampire, a terrible creature with burning eyes and great teeth which could have torn him into shreds. The experience had changed his life. The vampire had frightened him so much that for a long time Bert hadn't been able to go out after dark – not even to take Mrs Bungle to Bingo – and he knew he would never be able to rob another house. He would be far too busy looking back over his shoulder, wondering if the vampire was creeping up on him again.

In the end, Bert had moved to the country and become a poacher. This way he would still be stealing, and everybody knew that there weren't any vampires in the country. Unfortunately, everybody had been wrong. It was while he was out poaching that Bert had bumped into Fenella again, and this time it was even worse. Apart from being scared out of his wits, Bert had spent several days hanging from the top branch of an oak tree while woodpeckers pecked holes in his legs and squirrels stuffed acorns into his ears.

In short, Bert had met enough vampires to last him a lifetime and if he never, ever met another one, this would still be too soon. For several months after his second adventure Bert hadn't left his house at all. In fact, he would still have been there now if Mrs Bungle hadn't kept nagging him so much.

'Bungle,' she'd say. 'It's high time you got off your fat backside and did something. You make the house untidy sitting around here all day.'

'Besides,' she'd add. 'We need the money. Somebody's got to pay for my bingo.'

'But what can I do?' Bert had wailed. 'You know I can't go back to burgling.'

'Haven't you ever heard of W-O-R-K. Go out and get yourself a job.'

'Never,' Bert had said.

No Bungle had ever worked. They had all lived by thieving and Bert wasn't going to break with family tradition. In fact, he didn't start to change his mind until the following Thursday. This was the day Mrs Bungle gave him one sardine for breakfast, one sardine for lunch and another for tea.

'What's the meaning of this, you crazy old haddock?' he'd shouted. 'Are you trying to starve me to death?'

'Sardines are very nutritious,' Mrs Bungle told him. 'Besides, you'll get two for Sunday lunch as a special treat.'

'But I don't like sardines.'

'I do,' said Mrs Bungle, 'and they're all we can afford to eat until you start earning some money.'

This was enough to change Bert's mind for

him – he simply couldn't face eating sardines for the rest of his life. Unfortunately, he soon discovered that getting a job wasn't easy. As the man at the Job Centre pointed out, you needed to have qualifications.

'Cauli what?' Bert said blankly. 'I don't grow vegetables.'

He never had been very good with long words.

'You miss my meaning, Mr Bungle. Let's put it another way. What jobs have you had before?'

'None,' Bert told him proudly.

'Exactly. And what are you good at?'

'Breaking into houses.'

'That's my point, Mr Bungle. There aren't many jobs for idle good-for-nothings who have spent their entire lives stealing.'

'Oh.' Bert was surprised. 'Are you saying there aren't any jobs for me?'

'I'm afraid not, unless you want to become a lighthouse keeper.'

'There wouldn't be room,' Bert said sadly. 'Our house is so small we can't even keep a dog.'

It took some time to make Bert understand, but when he did, he was enthusiastic. In fact, he couldn't think of anything better for somebody who was afraid of the dark and had a nagging wife. Bert had started work straight away and he had loved the job from the beginning.

'You definitely did the right thing, Bungle,' he said complacently.

As he was on his own, Bert had started talking

111

to himself. He had also moved his bed up to the very top of the lighthouse, right beside the light. That way it was never dark. He was there now, listening to the sound of the sea far below.

'Plenty to eat,' he said happily, 'but no sardines.'

'No Mrs Bungle,' he said even more happily.

'And, best of all, no vampires.'

'That's where you're wrong, Bungle,' a voice cooed.

Bert was so surprised he sat bolt upright in bed.

'Blimey,' he said. 'I never knew I could do a voice like that.'

'You can't, Bert,' the voice told him.

There was a horrible sinking sensation in Bert's stomach as he realized the voice was coming from the shadows at the top of the stairs. Worse still, it was a voice he recognized. Peering into the darkness, he thought he could see the glint of red eyes and the flashing of great white teeth.

'Go away,' he whispered. 'Please go away and leave me in peace.'

'I can't,' Fenella told him from the darkness. 'I need you to do something for me, Bert. Why don't you come over here so I can talk to you properly.'

'No, I won't. I won't.'

'In that case I'll have to switch off the light and

come up to you. Is that what you want, Bert?'

It most definitely wasn't. Slowly, trembling all over, Bert got out of bed and started walking towards the stairs.

Seven

'It's very dark,' Igor said nervously.

'That's just what we want,' Bert told him. 'That way nobody can see us.'

Better still, he couldn't see Igor. Even the smell wasn't too bad if he kept upwind of him. Surprisingly, Bert wasn't at all nervous himself. In fact, it was rather like the good old days when burgling had been his life. Bert didn't have to worry about vampires creeping up on him because he knew exactly where Fenella was. She was waiting outside the garden gate, ready to come to his assistance if she was needed.

'It was nice of you to agree to help,' Igor whispered, following Bert as he tiptoed along the grass beside the path.

'I'm like that,' Bert told him. 'Always ready to lend a helping hand to anybody.'

He kept his fingers crossed as he said this. Bert didn't like helping anybody except himself but Fenella hadn't left him with any choice. She had told him that if he didn't agree to break into Mrs

Potion's house, she would be bringing all her friends to visit him at the lighthouse. Besides, she had promised that if he did this one job for her, she would never, ever bother him again. He wouldn't have to see another vampire for the rest of his life.

'Aren't you scared?' Igor asked, still speaking in a whisper.

'Me scared?' Bert laughed under his breath. 'Us Bungles don't know the meaning of fear. Besides, this is a real doddle. There's only one little old lady in the house and she doesn't even have a telephone.'

And there was a dirty, great vampire waiting to help him if she was needed. He didn't see how anything could possibly go wrong.

'I know, Bert, but this little old lady is a—'

Igor stopped because this was exactly what Bert had done, stopped so suddenly that Igor had bumped into him. They had reached the end of the path and Mrs Potion's house loomed in front of them, large and menacing in the darkness. Igor shivered at the sight because he knew what was waiting for them inside. Bert didn't and this was why he was so brave. Fenella hadn't bothered to mention that the little old lady was the Witch Griselda.

'Right,' Bert whispered. 'Here's what we'll do. We'll work our way round to the back of the house. Then I'll open a window for us.'

'OK,' Igor whispered back, trying to stop his teeth from chattering.

'And remember, keep quiet,' Bert warned him. 'Don't make a sound.'

Igor stuffed a filthy handkerchief between his teeth to stop them clicking together if they did chatter, and stumbled after Bert. He was even more frightened than when Samuel made him test one of his inventions. The thought of what Griselda might do if she caught him absolutely terrified Igor but he never once considered turning back. Sara was the only human friend he had ever had. She was the only person who had ever played with him. No matter what the risk to himself, Igor was determined to save her if he could.

Although it was dark and he had never been to Mrs Potion's house before, Bert moved quickly and confidently. He had been in countless dark gardens before. He had lost count of the number of little old ladies he had robbed. In fact, Bert was thoroughly enjoying himself.

Perhaps I'll go back to being a burglar, he thought happily. After all, it's what I do best.

Then Bert suddenly stopped, making Igor bump into him again. He had seen something in the darkness ahead, several somethings which almost covered the back lawn. It took him several seconds to realize they were statues, about thirty of them. All of them were children except for

116

one which seemed to be a small dog.

'What would anybody want with them?' Bert whispered. 'The poor old biddy must have a few slates loose.'

There was no answer because Igor had pushed past him, lurching forward to the nearest of the statues. The moon had briefly emerged from behind the clouds and Igor had recognized the nearest figure. It was Sara and yet it wasn't. When he ran his fingers over her face, all he felt was cold, hard stone. Beside her stood the small stone figure of Spot. Igor sniffed and wiped his nose with the back of his hand. It seemed Sara was in even worse trouble than he had expected.

'Come on, Igor.' To Bert they were nothing more than ordinary statues. 'We can't hang around here all night. There's work to be done.'

He was already moving towards one of the windows at the back of the house. It only took a moment to force it open and, after Bert had helped Igor inside, he quickly clambered inside himself. Once the curtains were drawn, he switched on the torch he had brought with him.

'Right,' Bert said. 'What is it we're after? Gold? Money in a mattress? Silver candlesticks?'

'No, it's nothing like that.'

This didn't surprise Bert because the room certainly didn't contain anything which looked valuable. Mostly it contained mess. Old books and pieces of paper littered all the tables and

chairs, and one entire wall was covered with
bottle-filled shelves. A broken, old-fashioned
broomstick leaned in one corner, a black cooking
pot stood in another and there was a stuffed
raven hanging from the ceiling. Looking around
him, Bert couldn't see anything worth stealing.

'What is it we want then?' he asked. 'Junk for a
Boy Scout jumble sale?'

'We're looking for a book.' Igor was more
nervous than ever now they were in the house.
'It's covered with red leather and it says *Yu-u-uck*
on the front.'

Although this sounded like a strange thing to
steal, Bert wasn't really surprised. He had

learned you couldn't expect anything normal where vampires were involved. The bottles on the shelves certainly weren't.

'Lizard's Tails,' he read from the labels. 'Crocodile Toenails, Snake Scales. What would anybody need these for?'

'Griselda uses them for her spells.'

Igor was already busy rummaging among the books.

'Spells?' It was as though somebody had poured a bucket of icy water over Bert. 'What do you mean?'

'Magic spells,' Igor explained. 'They're the ingredients the Witch Griselda uses.'

The jar Bert was holding slipped from his fingers and several newt's eyeballs rolled across the floor like marbles.

'A witch?' Bert squeaked, all the hairs on his head standing on end. 'Are you telling me the little old lady upstairs isn't a schoolteacher or Prime Minister on anything like that?'

'Of course not. She's a witch.'

Igor was too intent on finding the spellbook to pay much attention. The sooner they had it, the sooner they could leave.

'A real, live witch who can turn people into teapots or traffic wardens?'

'Or statues like the ones outside,' Igor agreed.

Bert opened his mouth to scream. Then he thought of waking the witch upstairs and very carefully used both hands to close it again. He was shaking like a leaf and he knew there was only one thing for him to do. Bert was halfway to the window when Igor grabbed hold of his arm.

'Where do you think you're going?' he hissed.

'I'm off,' Bert told him. 'I'm too young to be turned into a garden gnome.'

'You're not going anywhere. Neither of us is until we find the spellbook. Miss Fenella wouldn't like it if you ran off. In fact, she'd be most upset.'

There was no way Bert could win, not when he was stuck between a wicked witch and an angry vampire.

'I'll tell you what,' he said, his voice shaking. 'You check inside the house. I'll go and make sure the book isn't in the garden shed or the compost heap.'

'We stay together.' There was no way Igor was going to be left on his own. 'That's what Miss Fenella wants.'

As he didn't seem to have any choice, Bert reluctantly joined Igor in the search for the spellbook. Both of them were working at top speed, eager to be gone, but there was no sign of the book anywhere.

'We'll have to check the other rooms,' Igor said.

Like Bert, he didn't want to open the door which led to the rest of the house. There was no telling what might be on the other side.

'I suppose we'll have to. You go first.'

'No.' Igor was shaking his head vigorously, surrounding them both in a great cloud of dandruff. 'You're the burglar so you go in front. It's what Miss Fenella wants.'

Before Bert could begin to argue, he suddenly realized that neither of them would have to go through the door. There was a large table in the middle of the room and the floor obviously wasn't level because for the first time Bert noticed there was a book propping up one leg. It was a red leather book and when Bert shone his torch on it, he could see that *Yu-u-uck* was printed on the cover in gold letters.

'I've found it,' he whispered excitedly. 'It's over here. I'll—'

He had bent down to pick up the book and as soon as his fingers touched the cover it was as though a great shock of electricity passed through Bert's body. His hair stood on end, his eyes bulged in their sockets and he was thrown backwards to land in a heap. His entire body was shaking uncontrollably, his teeth chattering like castanets, and Igor had to help him back to his feet.

'It's all right,' Igor said once Bert had stopped juddering. 'I'll get the book. You hold the bag open.'

Thanks to Yu-u-uck's spell, Igor was un-

121

harmed when he slid the book out from under the table leg. Quickly he slipped the spellbook into the bag Bert was holding. Now they had what they had come for, Igor's only thought was to escape from the house while they could.

'Let's get out of here before Griselda hears us,' he whispered.

Unfortunately, they were already too late. With the spellbook taken from under the leg, the table was no longer level and, unnoticed by either of them, a large pile of books had been sliding towards the edge. Now they fell to the floor with a loud thump which made Igor and Bert jump. Worse still, almost immediately afterwards they heard the creak of floorboards overhead as Griselda jumped out of bed and started towards the stairs.

Bert had two great advantages over Igor. In the first place, he had been forced to leave lots of houses in a hurry while he was a burglar and he knew exactly what to do. As soon as he heard the noises from upstairs, he ran across the room, still clutching the bag, and dived out of the window. His second advantage was that both his legs were the same length while Igor's weren't. Normally, Igor made allowances for this and managed to travel in a fairly straight line. Tonight, though, he was too frightened to think properly. Igor was still running round in frantic circles when Griselda opened the door and switched on the light.

'Caught you in the act, pigeon-brain,' Griselda cackled, advancing into the room. 'You're going to be really sorry you ever came here.'

Apart from the flapping of the curtain, there was nothing to show Bert had ever been in the house. It was a different story for poor Igor. No matter how he tried, he couldn't get his legs sorted out and he was quite worn out with going nowhere.

'Stand still while I'm talking to you.'

As she spoke, Griselda clicked her fingers. Igor stopped in mid-stride, as though he had been quick frozen, his short leg still up in the air. Petrified, Igor watched as the old witch walked towards him, followed by her cat.

'Now, my little pigeon-brain, what am I going to do with you? Perhaps I ought to turn you into a tin of cat food and feed you to Scratch here. That would teach you to break into a defenceless old woman's house. Or should I—'

Griselda didn't stop because she had run out of nasty ideas. She stopped because, like most witches, she was rather short-sighted and she had only just come close enough to see Igor properly.

'My, my, my,' she said, her glare becoming a smile. 'Aren't you a pretty boy?'

Igor thought there must be somebody standing behind him. No one had ever called him pretty before.

'I didn't know humans could be so handsome,'

Griselda went on, reaching forward to pinch Igor's cheek. 'What's your name, my little pet?'

'Ig . . . Ig . . . Ig. . . .'

Igor was far too frightened to speak properly. Although the witch was smiling fondly at him, he could remember what she had said about cat food.

'What an unusual name,' Griselda cooed. 'Well, Ig . . . Ig . . . Ig, how about us making friends with a great big smackeroo?'

'A gr-gr-great b-b-big sm-sm-smackeroo?'

Poor Igor had no idea what she was talking about. He thought it must be special witch language.

'Come on, my pet. There's no need to be shy. You'd like to give me a little kiss, wouldn't you?'

Griselda had puckered up her lips, making her look rather like a gargoyle on a church roof. Although there was nothing Igor less wanted to do than kiss a hideous old witch, he didn't have any choice. Griselda clicked her fingers again; his neck muscles pushed his head forward; and, before he knew what he was doing, Igor kissed her.

'There, my precious,' Griselda cooed. 'That was nice, wasn't it?'

'L-l-lovely.'

It had been absolutely horrible, rather like kissing a dead haddock, but Igor didn't think it would be sensible to say so.

'I knew we'd get on together,' Griselda cackled happily, batting her eyelids at him. 'Now you're here, how would you like to stay? I could do with a handsome young fellow to help me around the house.'

This was an idea Igor liked even less than the one Griselda had had about kissing her. Once again, though, he didn't have any choice. When he tried to shake his head, it nodded instead. It seemed he would be staying, whether he wanted to or not.

Bert Bungle had never run so fast in his life and there was no saying how far he might have gone if Fenella hadn't grabbed hold of his collar as he rushed past. Even after she had lifted him from the ground, his legs kept working, running flat out in mid-air.

'The witch,' he panted. 'The horrible witch is after me.'

Fenella looked around quickly but Griselda was nowhere to be seen and there were no sounds of pursuit. Nor was there any sign of Igor.

'Where's Igor?' she demanded. 'What's happened to him?'

'It's the witch. The horrible witch has caught him.'

As soon as she heard this, Fenella's only thought was to rescue him. Dropping Bert, she started towards the house, only to run into the invisible barrier. It was as impenetrable as ever and she turned back to Bert. Although he was up and running again, Fenella overtook him with a few swift strides, grabbing hold of his collar again.

'Tell me exactly what happened.'

'The witch,' Bert babbled. 'It was the horrible witch.'

'I know all about the witch.' Fenella impatiently shook Bert the way a terrier would shake a rat. 'I want you to tell me what she did.'

'Ttthhheee hhhooorrrrriiibbbllleee wwwiii-tttccchhh hhheeeaaarrrddd uuusss.' The words

126

came out funny because Fenella was still shaking him. 'Ssshhheee cccaaammmeee dddooow-wwnnnsssttttaaaiiirrrsss.'

'And she caught Igor?'

'I think so.' Fenella had stopped shaking him and Bert was calming down now he had realized Griselda wasn't hot on his heels. 'As soon as I heard her coming, I jumped out of the window. I think Igor was too slow.'

'What about the spellbook?'

'The spellbook?'

'The book you went into the house to fetch. Did you get it?'

Bert was about to say no when he realized he was still clutching the bag in his hand. He had been holding it when he had heard Griselda coming and he hadn't thought to drop it.

'It's here,' he said.

Fenella eagerly snatched the bag from him and looked inside. She only needed to glance to know it was the book Yu-u-uck had described to her.

'Thank you,' she told Bert. 'You've done well. You can go now.'

'I can go.'

Bert could hardly believe the nightmare was over.

'Yes. You've done everything I asked you to do.'

'And I really won't ever see you again?'

'Vampires always keep their promises.'

Fenella was already changing into her bat form and Bert didn't hang around to say goodbye. He wanted to get back to his lighthouse, safe from vampires and witches.

'I didn't expect to see you again,' the cat said. 'I was sure Grisly would get you.'

'Well she didn't,' Fenella told him. 'Where's the wizard?'

'He's over there.' Fenella hadn't noticed Yu-u-uck curled up on the floor at the back of the cave. 'Poor old Yucky is exhausted. He needs all the sleep he can get.'

However tired Yu-u-uck might be, Fenella didn't think he would mind being woken up when he knew what she had brought. She went to the back of the cave and shook him gently by the shoulder.

'Go away,' Yu-u-uck mumbled, keeping his eyes closed. 'I'm asleep.'

'It's me, Fenella. I've brought you the spellbook.'

'You've got my spellbook?'

All thoughts of sleep forgotten, Yu-u-uck sat up. His hands were trembling as he took the bag from Fenella and looked inside. For a long moment he simply stared at the spellbook, tears sparkling in his eyes. Then he looked up at Fenella.

'You did it,' he said. 'You really did it. I'll never be able to thank you enough.'

Before Fenella had a chance to reply, Yu-u-uck leapt to his feet and began a mad dance around the cave, capering and cavorting as he waved the spellbook in the air.

'I'm a wizard, I'm a wizard, I'm a wizard,' he kept chanting. 'I'm a real live wizard again.'

'I think we've got the message, Yucky old mate,' the cat said.

Yu-u-uck didn't pay any attention and it was some time before he calmed down and stopped. As soon as he had, he rushed to the back of the cave and began hunting for a cauldron.

'Right,' he muttered, smiling fiercely behind his green beard. 'Let's get to work. Let's show Grisly who's the boss around here. She's really going to pay for what she's done to me.'

'You won't forget my friends, will you?' Fenella asked anxiously.

'Of course I won't.' Yu-u-uck stopped what he was doing to look at Fenella. 'I said all my magic would be at your disposal and I meant it. What would you like me to do?'

'Well, it would be useful if you could remove any spells Griselda has put on them.'

'I can't do that.'

Yu-u-uck seemed surprised by the request.

'Why ever not? I thought your magic was stronger than hers.'

'Oh it is. Much, much stronger. But I can't change spells she's put on other people. It's the rules of magic. I can stop her from getting up to any more mischief and I can cast a spell of my own on her but there's nothing I can do to change whatever has been done.'

Fenella was stunned by the news. She had been assuming all along that once Yu-u-uck had his spellbook back, everything would be all right. Now it seemed as though she had been wrong. If Griselda had already used her magic on Sara and Igor, there was nothing anybody could do to help them. Unless. . . .

'Wizard Yu-u-uck,' she said. 'You say there's nothing you can do to change any magic Griselda has already done.'

'That's right, I'm afraid. Only Griselda herself can remove her own spells.'

'She can't work any more magic on you, though.'

'Oh no. Now I have my spellbook back I can protect myself.'

'What a shame,' the cat said with a smirk. 'A few more flying lessons and you might have had your pilot's licence.'

The smirk disappeared when Yu-u-uck glared at him. He might still be in his nightshirt but the wizard seemed much more formidable now his spellbook had been returned.

'Could you do the same for me?' Fenella asked.

'Could you make a spell which would protect me from Griselda's magic?'

'Nothing easier, my dear, if that's what you really want. Mind you, I don't believe in half measures myself.'

As Yu-u-uck explained what he planned, Fenella started to smile. Perhaps everything would work out after all.

It was still dark when Fenella arrived back at Mrs Potion's house and on this occasion the anti-vampire barrier was no hindrance at all. If it hadn't been for the slight tingling in her wings, Fenella wouldn't even have known it was there. The house was dark and quiet and, from the air, the statues in the back garden were clearly visible. It was the first time Fenella had noticed them and they made her curious. When she landed beside them, she recognized Sara and Spot at once.

'Don't worry, Heinz Beans,' she said, reaching out to pat her friend's stone head. 'We'll soon put this right.'

Despite the comforting words, Fenella's face was grim as she walked away. At least the uncertainty was over. Now she knew what had happened to Sara and although it wasn't pleasant, it could have been much worse. Igor was Fenella's main concern now and for a moment she stared at the house, wondering where she would find him. Once she was inside, though, it proved to be remarkably easy. Vampires have an excellent sense of smell and Igor's familiar odour filled her nostrils as soon as she had stepped through the window. Moving as silently as any ghost, Fenella followed the smell upstairs and it led her straight to the small bedroom where Igor was. Although he was lying on the bed, his eyes were wide open. More surprising still, he didn't seem at all pleased to see Fenella.

'Are you all right?' she asked anxiously.

'I've never felt better, Mistress,' Igor answered in a strange singsong voice.

'Are you sure? Griselda hasn't done anything to harm you?'

'No, Miss Fenella. Griselda likes me.'

'That's a relief,' Fenella smiled in the darkness. 'You're safe now anyway. I've come to take you back to Blood Castle.'

'I don't want to go back, Mistress. I want to stay here.'

'You want to stay with the witch?'

'Yes, Miss Fenella.' Igor was still speaking in the same singsong voice. 'I think Griselda is lovely. She's the nicest, kindest lady I've ever met. We might even get married after she's dealt with the Wizard Yu-u-uck.'

Fenella realized it would be a waste of time to argue with him. Igor was obviously under some kind of spell.

'I'll come back and see you later,' she said softly, closing the door behind her as she left the room.

The witch's room was at the far end of the corridor and Fenella strode along it, making no attempt to be quiet. Outside the door she paused for a moment, allowing the anger to build inside her as she slipped on the goggles she had brought with her. It was high time somebody dealt with Griselda and she was in just the mood to do it. Throwing open the door with a bang, she stepped into the room and switched on the light.

At the best of times Griselda wasn't a particularly attractive sight but Fenella caught her when she looked especially revolting. In order to look at her best for Igor, the witch had put curlers in her straggly grey hair before she had returned to bed. She had also put on a mud pack and her face was a grey mask apart from where the odd wart stuck through. She sat up with a start when the door banged open, knocking the black cat to the floor. As soon as the cat saw Fenella, it retreated into a corner where it arched its back and spat at her. Fenella paid no attention to it. She was watching Griselda who was staring at her in disbelief.

'You're a vampire,' she said in her harsh voice.

'How clever of you to notice.'

'Well, if you are a vampire, you can't really be here. I must be dreaming.'

Griselda pinched herself hard with her bony fingers, making herself yelp with pain. Then she tried rubbing her eyes, making flakes of dry mud shower on to the sheets.

'I can still see you,' she cried in dismay. 'My vampire barrier must have stopped working.'

'It certainly didn't stop me,' Fenella told her.

'Pretty soon you're going to wish it had.' Griselda came out with an evil cackle. 'I'm going to turn you into an ant and then stamp on you. How does that grab you, bat brain?'

'You can do your worst, Griselda,' Fenella said with a shrug. 'You don't scare me.'

'That just proves how stupid vampires really are. Perhaps I'll turn you into a fly instead. Then I can pull off your wings before I stick a pin through you.'

'You can try, Griselda.'

With an angry scowl, Griselda muttered some magic words and clicked her fingers. To her amazement, nothing happened. Fenella was still standing in the doorway, completely unchanged.

'I must have said the wrong words,' the witch muttered angrily. 'Hang on a minute, bat-brain. I'll soon get it right.'

'You probably got it right the first time,' Fenella told her. 'None of your magic works on me.'

'Rubbish,' Griselda screeched. 'Absolute poppycock.'

She quickly gabbled another spell. When neither of Fenella's arms dropped off, her mouth sagged open in disbelief.

'I told you,' Fenella said. 'There's nothing you can do to harm me. On the other hand, there's an awful lot I can do to harm you.'

As she spoke, Fenella took three quick strides across the bedroom, grabbed hold of the front of Griselda's nightgown and plucked her out of bed.

'Put me down, you great bully,' the witch yelled. 'Otherwise it will be the worse for you.'

'You don't seem to have the idea yet.' Fenella had lifted Griselda so their faces were only a few centimetres apart. 'Without your magic you're nothing. You're simply an evil old woman who deserves to be punished and that's exactly what I'm going to do.'

'Keep those teeth of yours away from my neck, bat-brain,' Griselda shrieked, beginning to sob with fear. 'One drop of my blood will poison you.'

'I wouldn't dream of dirtying my teeth on a foul creature like you. I've got far worse in store for you unless you do as I say. You're going to remove all the evil spells you've cast since you stopped being a toad.'

'Never,' Griselda shrieked. 'I shan't, I shan't.'

'Oh yes you will.'

'I shan't, I shan't.' Griselda was foaming at the mouth. 'There's nothing you can do to make me.'

'We'll soon see about that.'

Fenella stepped across to the window and opened it. In a matter of seconds she had changed into her bat form and, still clutching Griselda in one claw, she stepped on to the windowsill.

'What are you doing, bat-brain?' Griselda shrieked, wriggling and struggling.

'I've heard witches enjoy flying,' Fenella told her. 'We're going for a little joyride.'

With great sweeps of her powerful wings, Fenella soared into the sky. Up and up she went, far higher than she had ever flown before, continuing until the air was too thin to support her weight any more. Only then did she stop. The ground was so far below them that even the houses seemed no bigger than pinpricks.

'Right, Griselda,' she said grimly. 'This is your last chance. Are you going to remove all those spells?'

'Never,' Griselda screeched, trying to spit in Fenella's eye.

'In that case, I'll be saying goodbye. I can't say it was a pleasure knowing you.'

It was a second or two before Griselda realized that Fenella had let go of her nightgown and that she was plunging towards the ground far below. As soon as she did, the witch quickly gabbled a flying spell and held out her arms. To her horror, nothing happened except that she was falling faster.

'I forgot to tell you.' Fenella was flying alongside Griselda as she dropped. 'None of your magic is going to work until you remove those spells. If you don't, you'll keep on falling until you smash to pieces on the ground.'

'Rubbish,' Griselda shrieked. 'I'm a witch. I can make all kinds of magic.'

First she tried a parachute spell. When this didn't work, she attempted a floating spell without any more success. She was still hurtling towards the ground and the houses below had grown to the size of matchboxes.

'HHHEEELLLPPP,' she screamed. 'HHHE-EELLLPPP.'

'Only if you remove those spells.'

'All right, all right,' Griselda babbled. 'Anything you like. Just stop me falling.'

'Not until you've done what I said.'

With an evil curse, Griselda began gabbling away, removing the spells as fast as she could. There were an awful lot of them and the houses below had grown considerably before she had finished.

'I've done it, bat-brain,' she yelled at Fenella. 'All the spells have been removed. Now will you save me.'

'In a moment.'

To the witch's horror, Fenella flew off, diving

earthwards even faster than Griselda was falling. Griselda screamed every foul word she knew at the vampire but it was no good. Fenella was soon out of sight and Griselda knew nothing could save her. Down and down she tumbled, faster and faster. The ground was rushing up at her with frightening speed, houses and trees growing bigger by the moment, and with a last curse Griselda closed her eyes. It was a great surprise, and an even greater relief, when a strong claw suddenly gripped her wrist.

'You didn't think I'd left you, did you?' Fenella asked with a malicious smile.

Griselda was too breathless to reply and she was still trembling a few seconds later when Fenella gently placed her on the ground. They had landed in the road near to the witch's house, directly under a streetlamp.

'Here,' Fenella said, 'before I go, I've brought something for you.'

She handed Griselda the piece of paper the Wizard Yu-u-uck had given her. Although she hadn't read it, Fenella knew what it contained so she wasn't surprised when Griselda started trembling again. Most of the mud-pack had been blown off the witch's face during the hair-raising descent and Griselda's face went very pale.

'Oh no,' she moaned. 'It just isn't fair. Not another seven hundred boring years of hopping and hiding under stones and—Croak. Croak.'

With a puff of smoke Griselda disappeared, to be replaced by a fat toad squatting on the pavement. For a moment Fenella felt sorry for her. Then she remembered all the awful things Griselda had done and her heart hardened. Besides, she still had things to do. With one last glance at the toad, she started off down the road towards the house where Griselda had used to live.

Ungrateful bat, Griselda thought, watching her go. After all I did for her, this is how she repays me.

Her mistake had been that she was too nice, Griselda decided. Next time she was a witch that would all change. Then she would be really, really wicked. First of all, though, she had to go and visit Alan Prince at 32 Blunsdale Road. Getting there shouldn't take more than twenty years hard hopping.

It was difficult for Sara to say exactly when she stopped being a statue. It was like having a vivid dream, then suddenly waking up in the middle. One moment she was simply a lump of stone on Mrs Potion's lawn. The next the horrible cold feeling was completely gone. Sara was herself again. She could move and talk and feel. It was a wonderful sensation and Sara bent down to stroke Spot who was excitedly jumping up and down beside her. All around Sara the lawn was filled with other children undergoing the same experience, chattering and laughing as they asked each other what had happened. But the other children didn't stay long. Very soon they started running off, eager to get back to their homes and loved ones.

Sara wanted to see her dad too, but there was someone else she had to see first. She stayed on the lawn with Spot after the other children had gone, knowing she's wouldn't have long to wait. Nor did she. As soon as she saw the tall, dark figure hurrying along the path, Sara started running towards Fenella, arms outstretched. As they hugged each other, their eyes were moist.

'I knew you'd come and rescue me, Fenella. I just knew it.'

'I'm sorry it took so long, Heinz Beans. I would have been here sooner if I could.'

'You came, that's the important thing. What did you do to the witch?'

'I taught her a few lessons,' Fenella said. 'You won't be seeing her again.'

'I'm glad.' Sara shivered and cuddled even closer to Fenella. 'It was terrible when I realized she was a witch. I only just managed to blow the whistle.'

'Don't you think about it,' Fenella said comfortingly. 'It's all over now.'

'What about Igor? Was I dreaming or did I see him while I was a statue?'

'You weren't dreaming,' Fenella told her. 'In fact, if it hadn't been for Igor, you'd still be a statue. The witch caught him too but he'll be all right now. Do you want to come inside the house with me to see him?'

'Please, but I mustn't be too long. Dad will be worrying about me.'

With Fenella leading the way, they went into the house and up the stairs to Igor's room. He was still lying on the bed but now his eyes were closed and he was sleeping peacefully.

'Poor old Igor,' Fenella said with an affectionate smile. 'What with one thing and another, he must be completely worn out. We'd better not wake him.'

'Would it be all right to give him a thank you kiss?' Sara asked.

'I think he'd like that.'

The little girl leaned forward and kissed Igor gently on the forehead. Although his eyes didn't open, a big smile spread across his sleeping face. It wasn't often that Igor was kissed and then it was usually by some ugly old witch.

'Isn't he sweet?' Sara said fondly. 'I do hope he'll be all right.'

'He will be.'

Fenella knew because it was something she had checked. This was why she had left Griselda while the witch was falling out of the sky.

'I suppose I'd better be going home,' Sara said.

'Dad must be wondering where I am.'

'Do you want me to come with you?'

'No thanks, Fenella – it's only just up the road. You will come and visit me again soon, though, won't you?'

'Of course I will.'

They went downstairs together and at the door they gave each other a last hug while Spot jumped up and down, licking both of them. After they had gone, Fenella went back upstairs to Igor. He looked so peaceful it seemed a shame to disturb him and she carefully began to tie the blankets around him. If she made a cradle out of them, she could fly Igor back to Blood Castle while he was still asleep.

It was almost daylight when Fenella finished telling Samuel everything that had happened. It had been a long night and Fenella was feeling tired. When she yawned, her mouth looked like a small cave with teeth.

'Well, at least it's all over, dear,' Samuel said.

'Yes, Uncle. I don't think we'll have to worry about Griselda any more.'

Fenella yawned again, wider this time.

'And I think you ought to stay here in the spare coffin for the day. You've done more than enough for one night.'

'You're probably right, Uncle.'

Arm in arm, the old vampire and his niece walked down to the dungeons. Once she had made sure Samuel was tucked safely away for the day, Fenella went across to the spare coffin. She knew she was going to sleep well but she didn't lie down immediately. There was a nagging thought at the back of her mind that something was wrong and Fenella sat there in her coffin, wondering what it was.

'I've forgotten something,' she muttered irritably. 'There's something I ought to have done that I haven't.'

For the death of her, Fenella couldn't think what this could be.

'Oh well,' she said. 'It's sure to come back to me tomorrow night.'

She was to remember long before that. Fenella

was still closing the coffin lid when she heard Igor shouting in the distance.

'THAT DRATTED GROTTIMO IS AT IT AGAIN.' Although Igor was a long way away, his outraged bellow carried clearly to Fenella. 'HE'S HAUNTING ME AGAIN WHEN I'M DRAT-TED WELL TRYING TO SLEEP.'

'Oh no,' Fenella groaned. 'That's what I forgot. I didn't ask Yu-u-uck to do his ghost spell.'

Wearily, Fenella started to climb out of the coffin again. Tired as she was, it was best to fly back to the wizard's cave and get it over and done with straight away. Then perhaps they could all have some peace and quiet.